THE STITCHER

Eccl 7:2

Ryan Barth

THE STITCHER

Ryan J Slattery

ISBN- 13: 978-1508738718
ISBN- 10: 1508738718

For Timothy Slattery

Contents

THE HARVEST

Erik admired the way his little brother could smile through his bloodied face.

Ozzie received a beating with all the regularity of a clock striking twelve, but this time it actually came at midnight. Ozzie crushed stalks of wheat as he fell, but he jumped up and struck back. He was no match for Jonas though. Ozzie was only eleven; Jonas was fifteen. And with four more years of hard farming labor, Jonas' arms were twice his size and impacted his body like an axe to a tree. Jonas' fist drove into Ozzie's gut and he dropped to the ground again.

The skin on Erik's face burned. His stomach clamped every time his brother got beaten, mainly because it was his fault. If it wasn't for him, they wouldn't be there. He dug his hand in his pocket, found his rock and squeezed. There was no chance Erik could best Jonas, but Ozzie was all he had left. He released the stone and lunged at Jonas. He beat his fat stomach, but it was like hitting a gorilla. Jonas grabbed Erik's arm and twisted. Erik shouted and dropped to his knees. Jonas kicked his stomach. The air shot out of him. He rolled into a ball on the ground and choked for air.

"You idiots want another round or you gonna get back to work? Dad won't be happy if the harvest isn't done before the storms come," Jonas said.

Erik struggled to his feet. Jonas deserved a beating of his own, but Erik was just glad the fight between Ozzie and Jonas was over. It cost him a bloody lip and the air getting kicked out of him, but it was worth it, for Ozzie's sake.

Jonas was right about one thing, though; a big rain could ruin the wheat harvest. But it would only take three or four more hours to do.

"We'll finish just fine. You just worry about yourself, Jone-ass." Erik staggered toward his brother. "Me 'n Ozzie work twice as hard as you anyway, and Uncle Bauer knows it."

"A wuss and an idiot is all you are, and *that's* what Dad knows."

"Just get back to work before we all get a beating," Erik said.

Jonas flicked his wrist and strutted off. "I already did my part. See you rats later."

"Where d'ya think you're going?"

"I gotta date with Lara tonight, not that it's any of yer business."

Erik smiled.

"A pretty girl like that…" Ozzie stammered between breaths, "ain't gonna go for a moron like you." But Jonas was already gone.

Erik approached his brother and shook his head when he saw Ozzie's smile, like pearls in a stream of blood. "What's wrong with you? Fighting him ain't gonna do no good." He pulled Ozzie up. "You gotta stop getting him angry."

Ozzie brushed his pants. "I didn't even do anything. He just wants to be a tough guy. Someone's gotta do something about it."

Erik patted down Ozzie's shoulders, brushing off dirt and broken wheat stalks. "Don't worry about that, he's in for quite a surprise when he gets to Krause's barn."

Ozzie wiped his mouth with the back of his arm. "Why's that?"

Erik laughed. "You wanna get back at Jonas? You gotta know his weak spot. Lara. I once heard him singing about her hair smelling like dandelions. It's pathetic. You know big Frieda? I got her to write a letter pretending to be Lara. It says she's always had a secret love for him and that he should go over to their barn tonight because she's got something special for him."

Ozzie chuckled and picked up his scythe. "How'd you get her to do that for ya? Did ya pay her?"

Erik followed his brother's lead and continued harvesting. "I've been saving up money just to get back at Jonas, but Frieda did it for free!"

"Why?"

"Guess she don't like being called *fatty* all the time and having her name written on their pigs!"

"Stupid jerk! Serves him right, I think he busted my leg."

Ozzie staggered as he cut the grain, but Erik couldn't do anything about that. He'd defend Ozzie the only way he knew how, but he was only fifteen. What could he do against the violence of this place? Could the stars defend the night from darkness?

Beyond Ozzie was the path into Odenwald Forest. It may come to that, but not yet. Over the forest flashed a small light, like a single shining hair. The wind carried a black cool to Erik's skin. The storm was coming early.

"We better get done fast, Ozzie."

Erik lifted Ozzie onto his straw bed. The smell of pigs and chicken filth hung in Erik's nostrils. The rain hitting the roof and occasional thunder made him glad to be back inside the barn. It was only 2 A.M. Uncle Bauer wouldn't be happy the harvest wasn't finished, even if the storm did come early. Maybe he'd take it easy on Ozzie, though. He was already plenty bruised.

"We're in for a beating, aren't we?" Ozzie asked.

Erik spread a ragged sheet over his brother. Wings flapped in the rafters. Some kind of bird was watching them again, for the fifth day in a row. "Maybe we'll be lucky," he said, looking down at Ozzie. "Maybe he'll just take away our food for the day."

THE STITCHER

"I think I'd rather get breakfast and a few lashes," Ozzie said.

Erik shook his head and looked over Ozzie's purple skin. "So what was this all about, Ozzie? Did Jonas say something about Mom again?"

"No. Nothing like that. I asked him about the Walter twins."

"The ones from Fulda? The ones that got kidnapped?"

"Yeah. I wanted to know what happened to 'em. He told me a monster got 'em."

"That's what Uncle Bauer said, but why'd he wanna fight about it?"

Ozzie smirked. "I told 'im if I'd been there, I woulda beat the monster off with my bare hands."

Erik chuckled. He didn't doubt it either. "Sometimes I can't tell if you're really brave or just stupid. Do you even know what kind of monster that thing was?"

Ozzie shook his head. "Jonas didn't say. But he was eager to fight about it."

Erik sat down and waved his hands in front of their eyes like he was opening a window. "Imagine a giant black bear, only instead of a bear's head it has two wolf heads stitched on top. And running down the spine are the dead heads of deer with no eyes and long antlers. Each paw was stitched over with snake-skin and each claw replaced with snake fangs."

Ozzie's face whitened.

"But, I'm sure you could handle it with your bare hands," Erik said.

"That's what took the Walter twins?" Ozzie asked.

Erik nodded. "Two heads for two children."

Ozzie murmured, "I still woulda tried."

Erik glanced again at the eavesdropping bird. He knew Ozzie meant it too, and that's what scared him the most. How could he protect someone braver than he was?

Erik stood alone. Trees surrounded him like a crowd of strangers around a lost child. Fragments of moonlight escaped between branches overhead, their shadows dancing in the wind. Or were they? Erik swore the trees themselves were crawling closer. But one tree never moved. It was the same pale blue as his eyes. It glowed against the dark night. Its roots traveled far into the ground, and reached Erik's feet.

Erik shoved his hand into his pocket. There was nothing there. He shook his hand around but it was completely empty. He searched his other pocket. Again, nothing. A trickle of cool sweat ran down the side of his chest. His face went hot against the cold wind. His nose tingled. He dropped to the ground and cast out his hands for his rock. Where was it? There was nothing there. He beat the ground. His fists felt red with heat. He tasted dirt as it flew in the air. The sound of stretching rope filled his mind.

Erik woke to a knocking on the barn door. He shook his head to break his daze. He felt the outside of his pocket; his rock was there. He let out a sigh. That dream again. The rapping came harder. Ozzie didn't stir; he just kept snoring like the pigs he slept next to.

Erik cracked the door and saw Jonas hunched over, arms crossed over his chest. His hair was unruly and his clothing unchanged from last night. Behind him it was still dark and the morning sun had not yet colored the trees of Odenwald with its orange and red light.

"Are you still gonna do it?" Jonas asked.

Erik eyed him. "What're you talking about?"

"Don't play dumb. I see you staring into Odenwald day and night. You don't think I forgot, do ya?"

Erik shook his head. He'd been foolish to trust him. "I thought I was doing you a favor, you filth." Who wouldn't want to run away from Jonas' father? A violent drunk with patience the size of a gnat's pinky toe. "Thanks to you those dreams are gone."

Jonas scoffed. "I did you a favor! You get food here, shelter, and 'good, honest work,' as my father says. Besides, d'ya really think you'd have survived out there alone? Odenwald is dangerous."

Uncle Bauer had told stories of fighting bears with nothing but his cutlass. Every time he went on a hunting trip, he'd come home with some new story of him or Krause killing some wild animal. Erik wouldn't have believed any of it if it weren't for all the animal heads he brought home. "How would you know? It's not like Uncle Bauer ever took you out there."

Jonas' face went red. "Like I give a shit. I don't have to go hunting to know you and dumbass wouldn't last a night out there, not without someone who knew how to fight."

"You mean someone like you?"

Jonas nodded.

Erik's nose tingled and his fingers and toes tightened. He was right; the forest was dangerous, but Steinau was a dangerous place too. Ozzie's eye was proof enough of that. Four years ago he spilt a bottle of Uncle Bauer's ale. Uncle Bauer'd been drinking and was pissed. He smashed poor Ozzie with a broken dresser leg. The stupid brute nearly killed him. His face was damaged and he lost most his vision in his left eye. Erik was helpless to protect Ozzie then, so he ran, hid under the hay, and cried. He'd plotted to run away from that moment on. He thought Jonas would be excited to be in on the plan. He received just as many bruises as anyone, after all. But like a dog returning to eat its own vomit, he'd told his father of the plan.

"We're not going anywhere," Erik said. "Those were childish plans anyway. Never woulda worked."

"Don't lie to me. I saw someone outside the barn last night. My father kn—"

"Are you crazy? Ozzie and I were dead tired from doing all the work last night, no thanks to you. We certainly weren't outside the barn in the storm."

Jonas' eyes narrowed. "I saw something. Don't think we're not watching you."

"You talk like you two're a team or something. He doesn't give a shit about you."

Jonas shook his head. "Yer as stupid as yer brother. I know yer planning on running away. You two won't last a minute out there without someone babysitting ya."

Erik clenched his fists and looked beyond Jonas. The forest looked still, peaceful; could it really be that dangerous? The mist between the trees seemed to whisper to his mind: *come and hide. Escape your life of fear.* It won't be forever. It's a road, a path to a new life. Erik had learned his lesson, though. Don't tell Jonas anything.

"Tell your dad we'll be feeding his pigs when he's ready to give us our beating."

Jonas looked down and scratched his chest. That was a familiar gesture. Uncle Bauer did that when he was sober and didn't wanna be. Jonas stood on his toes as if trying to peer beyond Erik. "How's, uh…how's Ozzie doing? I didn't break anything, did I?"

Erik shook his head. "It'd be a shame if Uncle Bauer thought your fight with Ozzie delayed your work," Erik said and closed the door.

Looked like Erik and Ozzie weren't the only ones worried about getting a beating.

Uncle Bauer hadn't smiled in years.

He also hadn't hunted in years. Erik and Ozzie followed Jonas into Uncle Bauer's trophy room, the only place you'd ever find him at home. The place gave Erik the creeps. The dead eyes of swine and deer on their hollow mounted heads seemed to observe their entrance as if some bloody liturgy were about to take place.

Uncle Bauer sat with one leg propped on his other upholding a smooth cutlass. Sharpened to hunting perfection, its polish glimmered in the candlelight. Erik knew each animal hanging on the wall knew that blade internally. But why was he polishing it now? He hadn't used it in years. Uncle Bauer's unkempt hair darkened his eyes and his beard made his whole face unreadable. His only movement was the rhythmic sliding of a cloth over the cutlass.

"Jonas, come here," he said. His words came slow, but without any slur. He sounded sober. Jonas slumped over to his father, his usual swagger replaced with the cowering of a begging dog. Uncle Bauer's hands moved swiftly down the sword. Jonas was now in striking distance. The cloth glided down the blade, then into the air, returning again to the metal. Jonas' head was down, his hands clutching his legs.

"I was out in the shed earlier today," Uncle Bauer said. "Do you know what I found?"

Jonas was silent. He shook his head. "The storm, sir. It…it came—"

"Dammit, I know. The storm came earlier than I told ya. But that wasn't my question."

Jonas spoke again. His words were almost inaudible. "No, sir."

Uncle Bauer straightened his legs and sat forward. He gripped the hilt of the cutlass and in one motion rested the blade over his shoulder, his left hand hanging between his legs. "I found some blood in the wheat stalks," he said.

Jonas' legs shook and he edged his head toward Ozzie. Uncle Bauer's head tilted up, his eyebrows furrowed as he looked his son up and down. Erik imagined Jonas' head on the wall over Uncle Bauer's chair. A chill shivered down his arms. Jonas needed a lesson, but not that. Still, it was nice to watch him squirm.

"That was an accident, sir. I…uh, me and Ozzie—"

"You two were fighting instead of working?" he asked. His hanging hand clenched around the rag.

"Y-yessir."

Jonas turned his head to the side, anticipating a backhand from his father's fist. It came with a crack. Jonas crumbled to the ground, holding his face. Ozzie turned away.

"Get up," Uncle Bauer said.

He did. "Yes s–s–sir."

"So you didn't see anything unusual in the forest then?" he asked.

Jonas looked up at him. "I…uh, no sir."

"Lots a strange talk 'round town," he said, relaxing his fist. "Folks talking about monsters called Stitches. They say they been coming out of the forest, taking kids."

Uncle Bauer resumed wiping his sword again. "Krause saw one himself. He said it had wings like an owl but an unnatural body. He reckoned it had more eyes than he knew how to count."

That wouldn't be too hard. Krause would have trouble counting his own fingers. "Do you believe him?" Erik interposed. "I mean, he's got that reputation."

Uncle Bauer's hands stopped and he glared at Erik. "Don't take me for a fool, you dumb bastard. I thought as much myself, but he wasn't drunk. 'Sides, even if he was it wouldn't explain his wounds. Something fierce came upon him."

Jonas rubbed his chin.

Uncle Bauer continued, "I told 'im if I were 'im I'd a—"

"Did he see it take any children away?" Ozzie asked.

What was he doing? You never interrupt Uncle Bauer, drunk or sober. Erik elbowed his brother. Ozzie's eyes grew wide.

"Where's yer manners ya puny dog. No *yes sir*, no *no sir* from either the two a ya. What can be expected from a couple ingrate orphans?"

"I'm sorry, s—" Ozzie began.

"Fer all I care he coulda been coming to take you two. Two less mouths to feed as far as I can see."

Uncle Bauer's face was red. He threw his towel to the side and scratched his chest as if some great itch came over him.

"I'm gonna be in town tonight on business. Lots a work to be done here tonight, though. I need all the wheat threshed and winnowed by the time I get home."

Erik shook his head. There'd be no way they could get all that done in one night. What was he talking about?

"And stay away from the forest; nothing good ever came out a there. Damn shame about the harvest. Shoulda never left man's work to a bunch a useless rats." He stood up, put his cutlass in his scabbard and left it on the chair. "It's gonna be one damned hard year."

A hard year for Uncle Bauer meant hell for Erik and Ozzie.

It was now or never.

THE ROAD TO LOHR

Three-hundred souls, some buildings and farms, Steinau was a small island cut off not by water, but by the ageless trees of Odenwald. Connected to the mainland of Germany only by a sliver of road to the east, the town was a bread-crumb in the maw of the forest.

Ozzie never entered Odenwald. Maybe it was the ghost stories Erik would tell, or maybe it was Uncle Bauer's fists that prevented him, but he'd made peace with Steinau. He had food, a place to sleep, and his brother.

After Uncle Bauer's interrogation, Ozzie walked with Erik back to the barn. He limped slightly from the fight last night, but otherwise enjoyed the cool air in his lungs and the fact that Uncle Bauer didn't add to the injury. It was nice to see Jonas get hit, too. He wouldn't have minded him getting a lash or two more for the trouble he'd caused. Every other step Ozzie took felt like a fresh punch to the leg.

"We got off pretty easy, didn't we?" Ozzie asked.

Erik didn't look at him. He stopped and watched Odenwald. "It's time, Ozzie. I know a place we can go now; Lohr. It's a large town about forty-five kilometers south of here."

The trees of Odenwald were colossal. He knew the forest was the path Erik meant to travel. Running away on the road would only mean getting caught and brought back to Uncle Bauer. The consequences for that were best not to even think about. Still, the forest was dark. Steinau wasn't so bad.

"Why now?" Ozzie asked.

Erik reached in his pocket. "He's gonna kill us, Ozzie."

"What? Uncle Bauer?"

"Did you hear what he wants us to do? It's impossible!"

"But he didn't even hit us today or anything."

Erik nodded. "He wasn't drunk. He's not going to town on business, Ozzie. He's going to the tavern."

"So? He gets drunk all the time."

"It's only a matter of time. Remember Aunt Beatrice? Uncle Bauer says she broke her neck falling down the stairs, but everyone knows it was him. Who knows when it'll be our turn?"

Ozzie hadn't heard that, but it wasn't too hard to believe, either. Uncle Bauer could be very violent, especially when drunk.

Odenwald loomed a kilometer away. Ozzie quivered as if an icy finger drew a line down his spine. Those monsters, Stitches, Uncle Bauer called them, terrified him. Uncle Bauer was scary too, but not like the unnatural creature Erik described. And why did it take children? No, he'd rather take his chances with Uncle Bauer than a monster.

"I don't want to leave," Ozzie said, standing tall. "It's not so bad here."

Erik stared at him.

Ozzie continued, "You just want to go because you're afraid."

Erik's look hardened, his teeth clenched. "It doesn't matter what you want. I'm the oldest and I say we're going. Tonight!"

Ozzie felt hot blood rush in his face. He shoved his brother, but Erik caught his arm and pulled him to the ground.

The smell of dirt and grass jumped to Ozzie's nostrils. It wasn't fair. He wanted to punch him back, but it wouldn't help. He pushed himself to his feet.

He had to stop this, but what could he do? Maybe just hide. Then they couldn't leave. But he couldn't hide forever. There was work to be done.

Maybe he could tell Uncle Bauer? No, that'd just lead to a beating.

Better yet, he could tell Jonas. After all, he was the reason the plan failed the first time.

Ozzie was a statue. He sat on his bed of straw, arms crossed. Since Erik was forcing him to leave, he wasn't going to do him any favors with the packing. Plus, he needed to stall to give Jonas time.

Erik moved quickly, folding a map into his bag, then packaging some dry pork and clothing. He lifted an empty crate revealing a package wrapped in newspaper. Mom's book of fairy tales. Erik had always wanted to read it, but Uncle Bauer said learning to read was a waste of time. There was always work to be done. Erik placed it snugly in his bag and continued darting around.

Erik glanced around the room, his gaze settling on Ozzie for a second, then on some rope. His hand hovered over it for a second, then grabbed it and put it away. What'd he need rope for, anyway?

"It's going to be a two or three day journey through the forest," Erik said. "Maybe more. It's important that we don't get turned around and get lost, so just follow me."

Ozzie was silent. He watched the door. Surely, Jonas would be there any minute. He'd told Jonas half an hour ago, having pretended to need to use the bathroom. Where was he?

From the corner of his eye, Ozzie saw something coming at him.

"Heads up," Erik said.

The warning came too late. A leather satchel slapped his face and he fell from the hay. He rolled on the ground where the chickens drop their waste. The stench invaded his nostrils. He spit on the ground and cursed his brother under his breath.

"About halfway between here and Lohr is an abandoned monastery. That will be our first goal."

Ozzie sat up and brushed himself off. He dug through his bag. A water container, some food, extra clothing, and some twine. All the comforts of home, except the freedom to stay. He glanced again at the door. What was taking Jonas so long?

Erik flung his bags over his shoulder and around his belt, clad with a couple of knives. "It's gonna get dark soon. We should get a move on before Jonas comes looking for us."

"We can't leave yet. I haven't even said goodbye to Bert yet."

"Since when do you care about the pigs? You've always hated them."

He was right, but Ozzie needed to stall. "They're not so bad once you get used to the smell."

"Shut up," Erik said. "There's no time. Let's go." He grabbed Ozzie by the shirt and dragged him.

Ozzie swatted at his brother. "Wait..." Ozzie stammered. "If we're leaving, why don't we get back at Uncle Bauer?"

Erik released him and looked around. "You mean, like, set the barn on fire or something?"

It wasn't Ozzie's best idea, but he'd panicked. Burning down the barn or breaking something could end up causing them more harm than good when Jonas stopped them.

Erik shook his head. "As much as I wanna get back at him, I don't wanna give him any extra reason to come after us." Erik grabbed him again. "Come on."

Ozzie wrenched out of his brother's grasp. "No, this is a stupid idea."

Erik took the rope from his bag. "It's for your own good," he said and tackled Ozzie, tying his hands together. "When you decide to come with me, you can walk on your own."

Erik opened the door to the darkened sky. Orange and pink at the horizon, the red sun was setting like a seed into the ground beneath the trees of Odenwald. He dragged Ozzie a few meters. Ozzie pulled against the ropes, but it was useless. He'd just have to hope in Jonas. He relented and slogged behind his brother. The shadows grew long on the ground. There was no sign of Jonas.

The forest before them was ancient and dark. Erik lit a small torch. Every step closer released a heavy ball in Ozzie's throat. He superstitiously avoided stepping on the shadows cast by the trees from the forest. The sound of fluttering wings shot from behind and startled him. He caught his breath. It was just a bird returning to its home. He exhaled and relaxed his hands. He didn't like to admit it, but the story his brother told him had scared him. Who made the Stitches? And why did they want children?

As a few trees passed by there was a rustling noise ahead of them. Ozzie's arms trembled. Fine, he admitted it, he was afraid to go. He slowed his steps and took a deep breath.

A shadowy creature leapt from behind a mossy boulder. Razor sharp teeth glittered by the light of Erik's torch.

"Going somewhere?" it said. The light from the torch revealed its face. Jonas grinned at them. The "teeth" he thought he saw was Uncle Bauer's cutlass, which Jonas brandished, swinging it like a stick.

Erik groaned and untied Ozzie's bonds. "Put that sword away, I don't trust you with it." Erik rested his hand on one of his short knives, not that it would be a fair fight.

Ozzie rubbed his arms, happy to see Jonas for the first time in his life. But what was he doing with his father's sword? It didn't really matter, though. With Jonas here, they'd surely be returning home.

"I'd love to see what my father'd do with you rats for shirking yer duties and running away," Jonas said. He walked toward them, smile widening and sword displayed.

Ozzie took a step back. So did Erik, who drew a knife, then another, handing one to Ozzie. "I'd love to see Uncle Bauer's face when he finds out you stole his cutlass." Erik mimicked the smile on Jonas.

Jonas' smile didn't waver. He withdrew the blade and hid it in the scabbard on his side. "Oh, he'd be angrier than you'd think." He removed a flask from under his coat. "I took most his ale too." He twisted off the lid and took a drink. He grimaced, but returned another smile and a laugh. "Got some bottles in my bag too, if you like."

"What're you doing? Uncle Bauer's gonna kill you!" Ozzie said. Beatings for breaking the rules came easy, but this kind of outright disrespect would bring a severe penalty. Ozzie rubbed the crevice in his forehead. He knew all too well.

"I'm showing what I can do. Maybe he'll learn he shoulda respected me instead of treating me like a dog," Jonas said. "Besides, I'm just doing what he did to me. I'm gonna take Meinhilde," he patted the cutlass on his side, "and show him I'm not some worthless rat."

"Didn't Uncle Bauer hunt with that sword?" Ozzie asked. He couldn't remember him using it in a long time. "When was the last time he hunted?"

"It was four years ago," Erik said. "The same year he smashed you with that dresser leg."

"It was also the year of the drought," Jonas said. "Bad business for Krause if you remember. He sold his hunting rifle for a week or two more of drinks, and Dad lost his hunting partner."

"So what? You're gonna show him how big you are by stopping us?" Erik said, pushing Ozzie behind him. "I've got no desire for my head to be on his wall."

Jonas laughed. "Don't be a fool. I'm not going back there! I'm going with you."

Erik lowered his blade and shook his head. Ozzie put his own knife in his belt. He hoped he wouldn't need it, but, big surprise, Jonas failed him. No, They'd be travelling through Odenwald after all. "Isn't anyone else worried about the Stitches, those monsters?"

Jonas bellowed.

Ozzie's face heated. What was so funny? Jonas might feel strong with Uncle Bauer's sword, but he was sure against a two-headed wolf-bear it wouldn't be all that more useful than his two fists.

"Stop it!" Ozzie shouted. "You'll be sorry."

Jonas recovered and shook his head. "Look dumbass, those things don't exist. My father made them up to keep you out of Odenwald. He knew you couldn't run away anywhere else without just being sent back, so he made up all kinds of crap to scare you."

Ozzie still felt the fire in his veins and shot back, "If you're so smart, then what about the Walter twins? Who took them?"

"There's no twins in Fulda. You ever been there?" Jonas asked. "Maybe there are and they died or ran away or were kidnapped. Or maybe it's just bullshit."

Erik spoke up. "Shut up, both of you. The real danger is Uncle Bauer coming home and looking for us. Thanks to Jone-ass here, he's gonna be pissed about his ale and sword, so our best bet is to get as far away from here as possible."

Jonas gritted his teeth, but agreed. He lit a torch and walked should to shoulder with Erik.

Ozzie followed them wanting to believe Jonas was right about the monsters, but as if from the setting sun, deep shadows of doubt expanded on the landscape of his mind.

Smoke wafted between the branches of the oaks. Ozzie thought he saw eyes peering at them from the branches, but he distracted himself by swaying a twig in and out of the fire. The smell of burning embers was warm in his chest in the chilly night. Jonas lounged, studying Meinhilde's shimmer in the light of the flames. Erik paced around the camp, tossing an occasional twig into the blaze.

"Sit down already. My dad ain't gonna find us way out here," Jonas said. "He probably won't even look for us."

Erik looked through the trees to the North. "With no work done and no ale, he'll be looking for someone to blame. You shouldn't have taken his liquor."

"Stop worrying. He'll probably go straight to bed," Jonas said.

"What if he doesn't? Did you ever think of that? What if he figures we left?" Erik said, picking up a branch and swinging it back and forth. "We should've gone farther before setting up camp."

Jonas glanced at Ozzie. "Does he always worry so much?" Erik had his hand in his pocket again. His pacing *was* unusual. Jonas joining their group certainly wasn't part of his plan.

"Besides," Jonas continued, looking back at his sword, "how would he even find us?"

Erik threw the branch at the fire. Orange embers shot into the air like burning dandelion seeds rising in a wind. "He'll know we'll need water. He'll know we are close to the river."

He was right. Uncle Bauer may be a bad uncle and a drunk, but he was a competent hunter. He also knew the forest better than any of them.

Jonas ran his hand through his hair. "We walked for three hours. Even if he does follow us, he'll give up sooner than that. And even if he don't, he won't run into us here. We're not even that close to the river."

"We're close enough for him to smell the smoke from the fire," Erik said.

Jonas scratched his chest. "You make 'im sound like a lunatic! He's not all bad, you know!"

Erik stopped. "What'd he ever do for us?"

"He hunted those bunnies for us."

Ozzie remembered that day. It was Easter. He was only five, but the memory was cemented in his

25

mind. Uncle Bauer had gone out hunting and arrived home with the widest smile. He squatted down and said he had gotten a special gift for each of the boys. Ozzie's heart had beat quickly, and he wondered what it could be.

A collection of dead bunnies.

It horrified Ozzie; their brown and grey bodies were painted with swashes of red blood. He'd never forget it. It felt so wrong. Something so weak killed like that. They never had a chance. He couldn't understand Uncle Bauer's joy, but it was Erik and Jonas' excitement that bewildered him.

Erik shook his head. "One day of kindness doesn't make up for the hell of living as his slaves."

Jonas hid Meinhilde and lay back pillowing his head with his hands. "Yer over exaggerating. He gave us food and shelter. We earned our keep, and our lashes. He'll be mad when he figures out what's going on, but he'll be in no state to actually find us."

For a while there was silence. Ozzie yawned and allowed the rhythmic cracking of the fire to lull him. It was hard to believe, but he actually agreed with Jonas. He didn't like being there, but at least they'd seen the last of Uncle Bauer. It was the eyes in the trees that worried him. Maybe it was just the fire in the eyes of innocent birds. Maybe they were just stars glimmering between the branches.

Erik and Jonas argued for a little longer, but it was in the background of Ozzie's mind now.

Something about the map, the sword, and Uncle Bauer. Ozzie wrapped a blanket over himself, clasped the knife on his belt, and gave in to the warm drift to sleep.

Erik stirred. Nightmares again. His neck ached and while tired, his heart was beating too quickly to relax. He rolled over and saw that Ozzie and Jonas were still sleeping next to a large stone. Embers glowed in the fire, now almost dead. The distant rushing of the river whispered off the trees. Thirsty, he sat up, rubbed his eyes, and reached into his bag. His bottle was empty.

The river wasn't too far away, and a quick walk might calm his nerves a bit. He stood and placed his knife in his belt. The forest was dark and the trees obscured the stars. He took a live ember from the fire and lit his lantern. The fire cast dim outlines upon nearby trees, rocks, and bushes. He inhaled the thin smell of leaves and smoke and walked to the sound of bubbling water.

He crossed over uneven stones, fallen trees, and brush. The terrain of jagged rocks and roots required his attention, but there was a faint fluttering that followed him. He stopped and held his breath, hoping to catch a glance, but when he rested there was only silence. Once he thought he saw the silhouette of an owl against the obscured moon, but it didn't make sense. What kind of bird trailed someone like that?

He knelt by the rocky edge of the river and splashed his face with water. It was freezing, but at least it distracted his troubled mind. He lowered his bottle into the rapids and filled it. Returning to his feet, the sound of nearby splashing startled him. Short angry spurts of mumbling followed. Erik bagged the bottle, snatched his lantern, extinguished it and crept behind a nearby tree.

"Where are you, little rat!" The uneven cadence of the voice jabbed a sharp hole in Erik's stomach. He'd found them! The water splashed again, closer. "Come on out. I know yer here."

WHHOOOSH, CRASH!

Erik's legs buckled and he tumbled to the ground. What the hell was that?

"Come out ya thieves." Heavy breathing filled the air as stumbling footsteps neared. "Ya think you can just steal from me? After all I've done fer ya?" His voice was close. The stench of ale tainted the air. Erik clenched his teeth.

WHHOOOSH, CRASH!

Erik shouted as shards of bark and wood showered over him. Uncle Bauer'd missed his head by a pinky's length.

"Ah! There's one little rat."

Uncle Bauer stumbled, half-wet, face white from the cold. His shoulders slanted like a balance weighed down by the large wooden dresser leg he gripped. His club had splintered and cracked from the two blows to the trees, but was still sturdy enough for more. The air filled with the smell of beer and cold sweat. Erik grasped for his knife, but Uncle Bauer kicked his hand, crushing it in place. He gasped and grabbed about with his other hand.

Uncle Bauer raised the dresser leg over his head. His face was veiled in shadows with only frightening pinpoints of light reflecting in his eyes.

Erik grabbed hold of a few small rocks and hurled them at Uncle Bauer. They pelted his face and he stumbled back. He tumbled over his own feet and crashed to the ground. For the first time Erik was glad his uncle was drunk. Erik seized his lantern and took flight.

After a quick sprint, he backed up to a rock face and peered back. Uncle Bauer's heavy breathing and lumbering stride gave his position and direction away. He was closing the gap. Erik needed to run, but he'd be leading him to their camp. It wouldn't work. He had to think of something. He shook his head and reached in his pocket. He grasped his rock tightly, hoping the pain would focus his frenzied mind. He peered around his cover again.

Uncle Bauer's pace slowed. Branches cracked on the ground beyond them both. Who was that? Uncle Bauer stopped dead in the forest and listened. Erik held his breath. Another twig crunched under the unknown weight. Uncle Bauer turned and muttered about rats making noise in the woods. He trampled off after the noise.

Erik exhaled, relieved his uncle was off his scent. Pain burned his wrist where Uncle Bauer had crushed it. But who made that noise? His pain transposed to fear. Had Ozzie or Jonas awakened and left to look for him? He grasped his rock all the harder.

He flew back to their campsite. Darkness still wrapped the forest, but dawn was not far off. Nearing the large rock where they slept, he heard the snapping of branches and grunting. The smell of blood was thin in the air. Ozzie tumbled on his back. His knife escaped his hand and clanked on a nearby rock. Jonas stood over him brandishing Meinhilde, blood dripping from his nose.

Erik whispered, "Stop you fools! What are you doing?"

Jonas startled, lowered the cutlass, and wiped the blood trickling down his face with his arm. Ozzie rolled over and picked up his knife.

"We're not alone," Erik said to Jonas. "Your father's here."

THREE BLIND MICE

Beams of sunlight broke through the trees and reflected off the pond. The watery grotto offered a cozy nest for respite. Erik removed his boots and dipped his feet in the water. Eight hours was a long stretch of travel, but they'd agreed to move on as swiftly as possible. Since Erik's near-death experience with Uncle Bauer, there'd been no sightings. Ozzie sat down next to Erik and unpacked some food, which he ate between heavy breaths. He had a couple scrapes on his face, but it was a deep cut on his arm that worried Erik. They'd tied a blue shirt around it, but now the make-shift bandage was dark red.

As Jonas wandered into the grotto, Erik broke the eight-hour vow of silence, "That's a bad wound, Ozzie. What were you fighting over this time?"

Ozzie looked at his arm. "Well, you were gone, so I woke him up and said we should go look for you.

He said it was too dangerous to split up and look for you. He said you'd come back."

"He was right. You should've known I'd co—"

"I thought a monster took you. I wasn't going to just sit there until you came back!"

Erik nodded. Ozzie must've still believed Uncle Bauer's stories. Erik wasn't sure, himself. Uncle Bauer might've lied, but it was hard to believe he'd make up a story like that. He just wasn't that creative. "So you tried to leave without Jonas?"

"Yeah. He grabbed me and told me to sit down, so I pulled out my knife an—"

"You did what? You attacked him first?"

"I was trying to help you!"

Erik sighed. Quiet splashes of water filled the forest. The water rippled around his feet. "It'll all be better when we get to Lohr. I can learn to read and teach you too. We won't have to be slaves anymore. Best of all, we'll be safe there."

Ozzie shook his head. "Not if we get killed by monsters first."

Erik kicked the water. "It's just a stupid my—"

"Hey!" Jonas yelled as he bolted out of the grotto. His eyes were wide as he bounded toward them.

Erik jumped to his feet. "What is it?"

Jonas unsheathed his sword, his eyes darting all about the forest. "There's a st-sti...There's a m-m-mons..." he stammered. "M-my father wasn't lying!"

"What?" Ozzie shot up. "What did you see?"

Erik pulled on his boots. So did Ozzie. They ran to the grotto, knives drawn. The air inside was cold, but mixed with the warm scent of rotting flesh. Ozzie gagged, but followed close to Erik. They crept forward. The tip of Erik's shadow rested on a hairy mound, about the size of a deer. Erik pinched his nose and knelt down, his knife cutting the space between him and the creature. Blood stained the rock floor. What happened to it? He slid his knife under the animal and lifted, but it was too heavy to roll. Jonas moved forward and pushed it over.

Ozzie turned his back, but Erik's gaze was locked. What would've made a creature like this? Its torso looked human, except it was covered with fur and stitching. It had no legs, but it had eight arms, like a spider. One arm was from a monkey, a few from wolves, and others he didn't know. The belly of the creature was scarred and stitched in zigzagging patterns. It had the head of a fox.

"It's dead," Erik said.

"What killed it?" Ozzie asked.

Jonas looked over the body. "I-I don't know. It doesn't h-have any deadly wounds."

With his knife Erik pricked between the stitching in its stomach. "It's rotting from the inside-out," Erik said.

Ozzie tugged on Erik's shoulder.

"Did you see anything else?" Erik asked.

Jonas shook his head. "I d-didn't see anything m-moving, but…" He lowered his head and cleared his throat. "There might be more."

Ozzie whispered, "Let's get out of here."

Erik nodded and they crept out. The trees looked different now. A moving branch meant nothing before, but now it seeded Erik's mind with concern. Hadn't he felt like something in the forest had been watching him? Where was that stalking bird?

"What're we gonna do?" Ozzie asked Erik. Ozzie's eyes were wet. Erik wished he'd never forced this on him.

"I'm going back!" Jonas said.

"We can't go back," Erik said. "Your dad's out there! He's trying to kill us."

"I didn't say you had to come with me. But I'm not going any deeper into this forest knowing that Stitches are real."

"We have to stick together," Erik said.

"You didn't even want me here in the first place. You should be happy," Jonas said.

"I didn't know the stories were real then. You're the only one with a good weapon," Erik said.

"Too bad. I'm going back. You can come with me or not," Jonas said.

Erik shook his head. Go back to what? Jonas hadn't seen his father last night. "We're not going with you. We're going to Lohr."

"No!" Ozzie yelled. "I'm not going with you anymore. I'm going with Jonas. I never wanted to leave in the first place."

Jonas smirked, which made hot blood rush in Erik's face. He clenched his fists. "We can't. Uncle Bauer's out there. He almost killed me!"

Ozzie stood next to Jonas. "I don't care. I wanna go home."

There was no home to go back to. The whole plan was to take Ozzie somewhere safer, somewhere better. But there was no arguing with him either. He'd made up his mind. Erik slid his hand in his pocket and squeezed his rock. He couldn't go on without Ozzie. He had to protect him. "Fine, we'll go back together."

The stop at the grotto didn't offer much rest. They'd walked all day and Erik's legs were stiff like wooden pegs. The rocky terrain tensed his muscles and each step propelled a shock up his leg and aching to his back. Erik slumped, while Jonas walked ahead.

"Slow down, will ya?" Erik said.

"We need to get back to the campsite before night. We don't have time," Jonas replied.

"We'll never make it," Erik said. "Besides, why would you want to camp there again?"

"Dad might look for us there," Jonas said.

Erik stopped. "We don't want him to find us."

Jonas travelled ahead apparently ignoring Erik's words. Erik trudged on, but quit half-step. Ozzie'd kept pace with Erik but smiled when Erik stopped and sat down.

They'd backtracked for a few hours and it wouldn't be long before nightfall. He dreaded the darkness of night, especially after running into Uncle Bauer. Jonas was hidden in the distant trees. Erik checked the map and compass.

Erik bellowed, "Hey, Jonas! What're you doing?"

Jonas stopped and turned. "Yer following me, remember? So follow or don't, but don't tell me what to do."

Erik double-checked his map. "You're going the wrong way. Come back here." They really shouldn't have been yelling. A cool breeze whistled in the air. Leaves rusted and wings of birds flittered between branches, but otherwise Odenwald was silent. Jonas slogged back.

Ozzie rubbed his eyes.

"We're going to have to take turns keeping watch tonight," Erik said. "We don't want to be ambushed by…" He tucked his map away, "…Uncle Bauer." He was going to say a Stitch, but didn't want to worry Ozzie, which probably wasn't possible anyway.

"That should be easy," Ozzie said. "I don't think I'll be able to sleep very well anyway."

"You'll be fine. I'll take the first wat—"

"Holy shit!" Jonas yelled. He bent down and retrieved something, but Erik couldn't make it out. Jonas came running brandishing what looked like a large tree branch. "You weren't lying were you?" Jonas asked, reaching the group.

"Oh no…" Erik said. Ozzie quivered. The splintered dresser leg lay still in Jonas' grip. Blood stained both the handle and the cracking end. Was it Uncle Bauer's blood or something else's? "You don't think he's—"

"Did you see Uncle Bauer?" Ozzie interrupted.

"I didn't see anyo—"

BANG!

The air quaked with the crash of a gunshot. Erik stood petrified. Jonas dropped to the ground and pulled Erik down. Ozzie mimicked them. The blast echoed through the trees. It was distant, but he couldn't tell how far. Jonas' eyes were wide and fixed on Erik.

"It couldn't be…" Erik started. "Krause?"

Jonas looked down. "Um…"

"You said he sold his rifle," Ozzie said.

"He did, but…" Jonas fidgeted with the leather strap on his belt. "Dammit, don't let it be Krause."

"But wouldn't Krause be able to help us?" Erik asked.

Jonas scratched his chest and reached into his coat pocket. He withdrew his father's ale and took a drink, wincing. "Not after what happened at his barn the other night."

"You mean the night of the harvest?" Erik asked. "What happened?"

Jonas put the flask back into his coat and exhaled. "I was waiting for Lara in the barn. She said she had something special for me. She was late, but I figured she was just getting prettied up. Y'know how girls are. Then the door opened an' in walked Krause with a rifle. He looked like someone peed in 'is ale too. He saw me right away. I nearly shit my pants. He shoved the butt of the rifle at me and said, 'what're you doin' here ya thief?' He thought I came in to steal his chickens or something. Then I did something stupid..."

Jonas took another swig. "I didn't want 'im to think I was there stealing. Then I'd get a beating from him *and* Dad, but I didn't know any excuse to tell. When I opened my mouth the truth came out. I told 'im I was there waiting for his daughter 'cause she was in love with me."

Erik restrained a grin. "Did you actually say that?"

Jonas chuckled. "Yeah. He was plenty angry, too. Lucky for me, he just gave me one quick thrust to the gut. Then he stormed off calling fer Lara. I doubt she got off as easy as me, though."

Erik's smile vanished. He never meant for Lara to get hurt from this. It was just supposed to be a joke on Jonas. He'd have to add her to the list of people he harmed.

"But where'd he get the rifle?" Ozzie asked.

Jonas swished the flask of ale, staring at it. "It's mine."

"Yours?" Erik asked.

Jonas nodded. "I've been saving up for it since Krause sold his. I thought I could be Dad's new hunting partner. But Dad took it away from me. Said I shouldn't be playing around with 'tools proper to men.' Then I see it in Krause's hands."

"He gave *your* rifle to Krause?" Ozzie asked.

Jonas pounded the ground and put the flask away. "Yeah, but two can play at that game." He smirked and rubbed Meinhilde.

"Do you think your dad and Krause are together out there?" Erik asked.

"I hope not. Krause knows I ditched the harvest. Dad'd kill me."

"Well someone's out there," Ozzie said. "And he's shooting at something. He might need our help. What if he's being attacked by a Stitch?"

"Hell no! If it's Krause, I ain't going anywhere near him," Jonas said.

Erik nodded and stood. "He's right. We gotta keep hidden." He pulled Ozzie up. "This way."

There was no fire. They'd agreed it'd be too dangerous. The wind frosted Erik's face and his nose oozed. Erik, Ozzie, and Jonas huddled together under a boulder that jutted over the earth. It sheltered them from the icy drops and gave cover. Erik's breath escaped as mist and mixed with the fog. His legs ached as if they'd sustained four bodies. Ozzie had it the worst though, since he'd limped for the last hour.

"I'll keep watch first," Erik said. "Four-hour shifts, then we move on."

"Okay, I'll go next," Ozzie said.

"That's fine by me," Jonas said. "Just don't wake me up until my turn."

"Are you actually going to sleep?" Ozzie asked. "I don't think I can."

Jonas scoffed. "What happened to all that courage? What about fighting off those monsters with your bare hands?"

Ozzie looked at his hands, then his arm. "We're not all as strong as you, picking fights with kids half your size."

"Shut up, ya rat! My dad's right about one thing. You need to learn yer manners."

"Would you two knock it off? The last thing we need is for you to start fighting," Erik said.

"Who made you the leader? Yer following me, remember. Feel free to find some other rock to hide under."

"Can we please, Erik?" Ozzie asked.

"No! We're safer as a group," Erik said. "Besides, he'd be lost without us. He nearly walked off in the wrong direction earlier. We need to stick together."

"I don't care if he gets lost. I only told him we were leaving in the first place because I thought he would stop you."

Blood rushed to Erik's face. That was how Jonas knew they were leaving? Ozzie'd told him? His fingers twitched. He thought Jonas knew they were running away because he was watching them. If Jonas hadn't come, Uncle Bauer might not have been so angry. His chest flushed with heat and he shifted his body.

Jonas grunted. "Dammit! What the hell's in yer pocket, Erik? Yer jabbing me in the back."

Erik's heart jumped. He turned back. "It's nothing, just something I forgot to put back in my bag."

"Well put it back in yer bag, I don't want it stabbing me in the middle of the night," Jonas said.

Erik's fingers coiled. No one knew about his stone, not even Ozzie. He shoved his hand in the pocket and squeezed the rock. "Just go to sleep," he ordered.

"I can't," Ozzie said.

"Close your eyes. Count sheep. There's nothing to be worried about," Erik said.

Wind screamed through the branches and rain pounded the rocks. Erik breathed deeply and relaxed his hand.

"It's not working," Ozzie said. "The sheep keep turning bloody. Will you tell me a story? About Mom?"

Erik gritted his teeth. "Fine," he said. What could he do? Ozzie's mind was troubled, and being in the forest wasn't helping. "But you have to promise not to say a word after it's over."

"Okay," Ozzie said.

Erik knew Ozzie loved listening to any story about their mother. Erik didn't know many since she died when Erik was five, but his dad used to talk about her, until he left too. "I was only three years old, but Dad told this story a lot. Mom was playing with me one night. Dad says she used to dance around with me when I was little. I don't remember it, but that night she started to faint. Her vision got blurry and her chest started to hurt. She didn't think too much of it because she was pregnant with you, but Dad wanted Mr Franke to check on her. He was the doctor. He came, listened to her breathing, checked her pulse, and asked her all kinds of questions. Dad was worried, and after Mom died, he said he always knew something was wrong.

"Mr Franke said she had something wrong with her blood. I don't really know what it was. He said women sometimes get it when they're gonna have a baby, but that it can be dangerous. That's when Dad and Mom had a big fight. Mom said it was nothing, but Dad wanted to fix it. After she died he always said he should've done something, but Mom didn't want to."

Jonas shifted. "Why didn't she want to fix it?"

"They thought her blood was like that because she was having a baby, so Dad wanted to stop her from having the baby."

Ozzie breathed slowly.

Jonas asked, "Why didn't he just stop her then?"

"I don't know. He used to ask that question a lot after Mom died."

Ozzie lay still. It wasn't the first time he'd heard it, but it was Jonas'. Erik knew Ozzie liked this story because Mom had protected him.

For a while, only clouds of mist escaped from anyone's lips. The rain trickled on stones outside their haven. Distant thunder crashed, but Erik never noticed any illumination in the sky. The dome of branches blotted out the light.

Ozzie breathed steadily. Maybe he was asleep now. Erik turned, watching the dance of rain on the rocks outside. Jonas let out a grunt that startled Erik and stirred Ozzie. Jonas yelled, "Stop stabbing me!"

Erik turned back, "Sorry, I forg—"

"Take that damn thing out of yer pocket now, or I'll rip it out myself."

"It's nothing. Stop yelling," Erik said.

"Not 'til you empty yer goddam pocket!"

Warm blood rushed to Erik's face. How could he have been so careless? He guarded his pocket. "Back off. I didn't mean to—"

A swoosh of wings cascaded and a thud cracked a branch beside them. An owl stood silhouetted in front of them. A sound came from the creature, a shushing noise. Ozzie gasped, and the creature spread its wings and returned to flight.

"What was that?" Ozzie asked.

Erik didn't know. It looked like an owl, but it didn't sound like one. Still, it didn't appear to be dangerous. "It's just a bird," Erik said. "Go back to sleep."

The pounding of the rain grew and ceased minute by minute. Before long, despite his fear, Ozzie snored softly. Hopefully tomorrow Jonas would forget all about the rock in Erik's pocket.

In the cool black Erik's eyes grew sore. They closed and he opened them. He hadn't slept well lately, but he was on first watch. He needed to stay awake. His eye-lids closed, as if drawn together by magnets. His mind drifted to the song of the storm. He opened his eyes, trying to startle himself to wakefulness, but sunk further to sleep.

Dead white. That was the color the moon glared, its rays encircling the blue tree. Erik approached it, pulling his hands from empty pockets. In the middle of the tree was a hole. Inside the hole he saw it – his rock. He reached in and grabbed hold, but it was fastened in place. He yanked it, but it still held firm, although the ground beneath him began to crumble into a pit.

He lost his footing and plummeted into the nothing under the tree. The roots caught him by the neck and strangled him. He struggled and pulled at the roots, pained gasps for breath retreating from his mouth.

Then he saw that he wasn't alone. Someone else hung, strangled by the roots. A white sheet hung over his head. Whoever it was, he wasn't breathing. Erik reached to pull the sheet off the man, his fingers hovering near the cloth.

"Get out of here! Run!"

Erik bolted awake.

"Arrrrgh!" Jonas cried. "Dammit Erik!" Jonas scrambled out from under the rock into the rain. He pulled out Meinhilde and pointed it at Erik. "Take it out! Now!"

The owl was back, standing behind Jonas. It spread its wings and soared away. Erik shook his head. Who was under that white sheet? Why did he keep having this nightmare?

Jonas inched the sword closer.

"I...I'm..." Erik muttered.

"Do you guys hear that?" Ozzie asked.

Jonas stood waiting for Erik's response, and more likely for him to empty his pockets.

"Yeah. What is it?" Erik asked. "It's getting louder."

Jonas' eyes narrowed and his head turned.

The muffled grunting, at first masked by the rain drumming the rocks, now rose like a wave crashing over water. Had Uncle Bauer found them? On a hill between the trees lumbered a black shape moving through the fog.

Erik shoved Ozzie. "We gotta get out of here! It's Uncle Bauer."

Jonas kneeled behind a bush. "Are you sure? That doesn't sound like my dad."

Erik stilled to listen. He was right. Low growling pervaded the air and seemed to echo from all sides. No, there were different sounds, one from beyond and one near. Erik's teeth clenched and his cheeks swelled with heat. He grabbed his knife, and jumped out from their resting place. "Ozzie, stay there!"

"What's going on?" Ozzie asked.

Before them bounded a shadowy movement in the mist. The forest echoed a short high-pitched scream. Erik cringed and narrowed his eyes. "It's just a fox," he said. He didn't believe that, but he hoped it was true anyway. "Just stay there. They don't usually attack people."

Jonas gripped Meinhilde and crouched. "I hope yer right," he whispered.

Erik planted his legs and tightened his arms. The creature's feet crashed into the earth, crunching leaves and branches. It was the size of a bear, but had a wolf's head. Its breath escaped from its mouth like smoke from a furnace, its eyes like red embers. Then he saw its twin: a second wolf-head. Erik's throat choked from the cold; his arms froze. His eyes were fixed on the creature, now only meters away.

Erik's head slammed into his shoulder as if hit with a club. Shrieking like thunder blasted his left ear. He toppled to the ground. His knife flew from his hand into a bush. He felt like Uncle Bauer had slammed him with that wooden leg, except that whatever hit him was still on him, howling and snapping.

Erik thrashed back. He couldn't roll; it pinned him. Its breath was warm and wet on his face and smelled of flesh and saliva. It clawed his chest and Erik beat it with his fists.

Jonas yelled. The creature's weight evaporated and it screamed like a train crying to a stop.

Jonas shoved it to the ground and stabbed the cutlass into its body. It screeched and jumped into him. It was smaller than Erik had guessed, about the size of a dachshund, but its claws were like knives.

He lifted a hand to his ear. The ringing persisted, but he heard two sounds as through water. One was a low growling, unlike the screeching of the creature that ambushed him. The second was Ozzie. What was he saying?

"Look out!"

He caught sight of it out of the corner of his eye. It was the bear. Its paw thrashed into his chest flinging him from the ground. He pounded into rocks. He lay paralyzed in black wetness. His fingers quivered, his head fell to the ground. Everything was moving but him. He choked and smelled vomit.

Ozzie screamed. His voice neared and seemed to be in front of him. Erik raised his head and squinted. Ozzie's shape was outlined in the fog. He held his knife out and stood tall. Beyond him the creature's shape rose and overshadowed him. Erik grasped for his rock, but he couldn't move. He tried to stand, but his face went cold and his legs limp. "Ozzie…" he whispered.

Then there was nothing.

EYES IN THE SKIES

Tiny eyes stared back at him. Thin black strips separated its almond-colored irises. Its mouth hung open stupidly. Its teeth were small but sharp. Erik startled, but exhaled when he saw the creature's head, because it was only its head. Dead, ugly, and lifeless on the ground.

"That's the one that almost ripped your heart out," Jonas said, laughing.

Pain lingered in Erik's chest as he labored to breathe. He felt like he'd been the rope in a tug-o-war between Uncle Bauer and Krause. He touched his ear to make sure it was still there, staring at the dead fox's mouth.

Jonas must've thought it'd be really funny to have him wake up and see that thing. "The fruit don't fall far from the tree does it, Jone-ass?"

"What're you talking about?"

"You think this Stitch-head'll look good on your wall?"

Jonas swiped the head. "You should be thanking me. This thing was killing you."

"That don't mean I want to see it first thing in the morning."

"Don't be such a baby. It was just a joke. At least yer alive."

Being alive didn't make acknowledging Jonas was right any easier, or his body feel any better. Jonas' pride in his head-hunting disturbed Erik, but at least it wasn't his own head that was ripped off.

Jonas pulled out his bottle of ale and drank. Did he really think he was sticking it to his old man by drinking his ale? Couldn't he have pissed him off just as bad by pouring it out? Maybe Jonas didn't see it, but he and Ozzie knew. Jonas hid the flask in his jacket. Around him were the usual bushes and trees, but nothing else...no one else.

Erik's chest quivered from the inside. "Where's Ozzie?"

Jonas wrapped the head of the Stitch in a rag and put it away. "He got taken."

"What? Why didn't you save him?"

"I was busy fighting off this one," he said, narrowing his eyes. "I didn't see you help him either."

Erik seized his rock. "I blacked out! What happened to Ozzie?"

"He attacked the thing, but it knocked him down. It looked like it was going for you, but Ozzie started slashing its back. It turned on him and stood up. It must've been part bear or something. It grabbed him and ran off. Ozzie was calling yer name and screaming, but there wasn't nothing I could do.

"After I killed the little one I picked you up and started running. I didn't want anything to come back for us."

It was surprising that Jonas didn't just leave him there and run off himself, but what about Ozzie? "We've got to save him!" Erik said, walking. His chest shot with pain with every breath and his back was stiff.

Jonas didn't move.

"C'mon! What'r'ya waiting for? Let's go."

"Did that thing knock yer brains out? Only thing for us to do is get outa here as soon as possible."

"What? You're just gonna leave Ozzie?" Erik's mind blurred red with anger and fear. He hated to admit it, but he needed Jonas' help. "You're turning out to be just like your Dad. You only care about yourself."

Jonas gnashed his teeth. His reaction wasn't at all what Erik wanted. He was angrier than if he'd found out the letter from Lara was really from Erik.

"Maybe I should've left you there then," Jonas said. "Then you and your idiot brother would be together."

It was hopeless. Erik walked a few steps. "Are you coming with me or not?"

"You don't even know where to go. Don't be stupid."

"I'll go back to where we were attacked. Maybe there'll be some clue there."

"You were out cold for hours. How do you expect to find that place again?"

Rocky terrain, trees, and bushes encompassed him in all directions. It all looked the same. "Well, which way did you come?"

"I don't know. It was dark and I was running. It's not like I stopped and asked for directions."

"What? You don't know where we are?"

"I was—"

"Shhh..." Erik raised his hand for silence. "I don't hear anything. Which way is the river?"

Jonas looked down. "I-I don't kn-know."

"Are you kidding? You're always yelling at Ozzie for how stupid he is and you just got us lost in the forest? How am I supposed to find Ozzie?"

"Shut up already. I-I'm pretty sure I came this way."

"I hope you're right. Once we find the river, my map will be able to point you home. I hope Uncle Bauer likes your stupid trophy." More likely he'll put him to work day and night until the work they'd skipped gets done.

Jonas mumbled. He pulled out the ale and drank it. His eyes were pink. Odenwald has not been good for sleeping. Erik couldn't wait to find the river. As much as he needed Jonas' help, he couldn't wait until they parted ways.

The grass was painted crimson. Markus' leg shook as he tied a tourniquet to stop the blood loss. This wouldn't end well. It'd get infected. They'd have to amputate. That's if he made it out alive. Where was his son? Was he dead? Nils had been gone for too long, he might not come back at all. He laid his head back against the tree and pulled out the gold.

He flicked through the coins in the bag. This was just the advance; there'd be more when they completed the mission, but now it looked like that wouldn't happen. He tossed the gold to the ground. It was of no use now.

Where was Nils? They'd split up to pursue a wild man that attacked them in the night, but he never saw either of them again. After waiting a half-hour he returned to the glade, their rendezvous point. No one was there. He'd waited for hours, but his son never returned.

But something else had found him.

The sound of wings had escaped to his ears. He looked up knowing it could only mean one thing: they'd found him. He raised his rifle to meet the creature and shot, but it was too late. The Stitch had flown off. His position was now compromised. He could run or he could stay and wait for his son. He took a minute to prepare his rifle for another shot. He checked his knives. He decided Nils wasn't coming.

So he'd run.

That was when he saw it; the largest Stitch he'd ever seen. It had the body of a black bear and two wolf heads. A young boy drooped, gnashed in its maw. Nils? He aimed his gun, but couldn't shoot. He couldn't risk hitting the boy. He withdrew his knife and lunged. It cracked into its skin like a blade upon armor. It felt like bones had been stitched under its fur.

It slashed into Markus' leg with razor-like claws. His bone snapped like a dried tree branch. The Stitch flung him with a sudden blow. Markus plummeted to the rocks. He'd begun to crawl, but the Stitch loomed over him. He scrambled and found his rifle. He pointed it at the beast and shot. Child or no child was no longer relevant.

By the time the thunder and ringing from the shot faded, he was alone. The Stitch was gone, and Markus had nothing better than to crawl to a tree and assess his condition.

His leg seized and shook. His gold coins were strewn in the bloodied grass, like tiny suns in the evening sky.

His arms grew cold. His breath was shallow in his lungs. A vulture cawed above him. He wouldn't have strength to fight off scavengers for long. The scent of blood might attract wolves, too. He'd have to find a better way. He pulled out a parchment and pen to take down his last thoughts.

Nils,

We came to right place. The Stitcher is near.

The reports are true.

Get out of the forest.

If you find me, I'm sorry.

Dad

Why was Jonas always right? Erik's plan to rescue Ozzie was like a jigsaw puzzle, except now that they were lost, it was like the pieces were all upside-down. Even worse, he wasn't even sure he had all the pieces in the first place. What took Ozzie? Where did it take him, and most importantly, was he even still alive?

Yet, what could he do but try and save him? Go back with Jonas? Be alone in the barn with the pigs and chickens? His mother and father were both gone; Ozzie was all he had left. Death would be better than slavery in Steinau with Jonas and Uncle Bauer.

"Does that mound look familiar to you?" Jonas asked.

A giant rock punched through the earth. Erik sighed.

"It's that same stupid rock," Jonas muttered. "It's the one that looks like a hand, again."

He was right, again, except it wasn't just a hand, it was a fist, pounding his spirit into the ground. "That's not possible! How could we have gone in a circle?"

Jonas dropped his gear to the ground and sat. "We still have a few hours before evening. I say we take a different path."

Erik dropped to the ground himself. He rubbed his calves. It felt like they'd been in a furnace. He took a deep breath. His lungs stabbed with pain. He never knew how much he missed something as simple as breathing. He dug into his pocket for his stone and seized it. Jonas wasn't watching, so he took it out. It was smooth but clunky like a hard potato. "What does it matter? We're not gonna find Ozzie. We can't even find the river."

Jonas jumped to his feet. "Shut up! I for one don't wanna die in this stupid forest."

Erik pocketed the stone, shook his head, and stood up. A familiar flittering of wings cascaded from above. The bird darted ahead of them. Was that the owl they saw last night? It'd been following them for a while. It was weird. It almost seemed like it had tried to warn them before the ambush. It perched just beyond the fist-shaped rock, away from any clear path. What was it up to now? Did it want them to follow it?

"I think we should go this way," Erik said, pointing past the mound.

"Why? Do you think you know where we are?"

"I gotta hunch."

Jonas shrugged. "Fine. It's as good as any way, I guess."

Erik tracked the bird through the forest, thankful that it never rested on a branch for long. It did appear to be leading them, but it kept its distance. Erik never got more than a glance at it. And Jonas didn't seem to notice they were following the owl at all. The last thing Erik needed was to explain why he was following a dumb bird. It was hard enough to explain it to himself, but he'd ran out of sane ideas long ago.

After a couple of hours the bird vanished into the trees and Erik stopped. Tall oaks and their maze of branches hid the owl. What was special about this place? Odenwald was forbidding and large as always, and after a couple days it all began to look the same. The green and gold of the leaves dimmed though. It wouldn't be long before nightfall.

"Why'd you stop?" Jonas asked.

He didn't know. He lifted his finger to his lips, requesting silence. He needed a minute to make up a reason that wouldn't sound crazy. It turned out he wouldn't need one. He heard it, faintly through the trees – the river! "Listen," he said. And for the first time since Ozzie was taken, a smile came to his face.

Jonas shook his head. "What is it?"

"Follow me," Erik said. He ran quickly, ignoring the screaming in his legs. The gushing of water grew louder.

"Is it the same river?" Jonas asked.

"It's gotta be. It's the only one in the area."

Running on the wet rocks, Erik stumbled, nearly falling into the water. He took large drinks from the river and splashed it on his burning calves. It couldn't quench the pain, but it still felt good.

The refreshment had been nice, but there was no sky left above them. The trees vanished into darkness. Erik's skin froze. He pulled on his coat, but the cold was the least of his fears. Surviving another night in Odenwald ranked much higher.

Nils fought with the ropes. His arms burned against them as he struggled. The binding was secure. He was as immobile as the tree he was tied against. The only difference was the tree had nothing to fear; it wasn't the one stuck with a maniac.

The man was wet with sweat despite the cold. His fingers and arms twitched like the death throes of an insect. But he was in control. He studied Nils' rifle in the light of the fire and pocketed the rounds.

Over the fire roasted what was left of the Stitch. It was part wolf, part deer, part fox, and probably more, but it was hard to tell. The smoke carried the scent to Nils. His mouth watered, but the thought of it repulsed him.

"What're you doing in the forest?" the man asked.

"I was hunting with my father," Nils said. "Until you attacked us."

The man's eyes grew wide and the veins on his neck flared as he yelled. "Show some respect you rat! You were chasing me, remember?"

"Yeah, okay, sorry," Nils said softly, doing his best to calm the man down. "We tracked you because we didn't know if you were friend or foe."

"Yer not who I thought you were anyway," the man said. He walked to the fire, took a knife, and sliced off a piece of barbecued meat.

"Who'd you think I was?"

"My son and a couple rats. Yer about the same age, though," he said, taking a bite.

Why would they be in the forest? He thought to ask, but decided it probably wouldn't lead to anything good.

"Wanna bite?" The man held out a sliver of meat impaled on his knife.

No, he didn't, but he wasn't in a position to refuse any offerings either. He closed his eyes and nodded, not trusting his mouth to speak the lie.

The man shoved the meat in Nils' mouth. He closed his mouth over the flesh and chewed.

"You seen anyone else in the forest?" the man asked.

Nils choked down the meat. "No sir. We haven't seen anybody since we came to Odenwald."

"What're you hunting here fer? Ain't you heard what's been going on in this forest?"

Should he tell him he'd come to hunt the Stitcher? Nils wasn't sure he wasn't talking to him right then. Better to play as dumb as possible. "Does it have something to do with that creature you're cooking over the fire?"

The man laughed. "It does. Rumor is these ugly things, *Stitches* people been calling 'em, are taking children into the forest. Some people think they're eating the poor bastards."

"Is that why you're here? To protect your son?"

The man's smile died and his fist clenched around the knife. He stabbed it into the center of the Stitch. "Ingrates!" he yelled. "I warned 'em about what was going on here…"

Nils knew only a couple things about this man. One, he was as dangerous as dynamite and just as explosive, and two, he was not the Stitcher.

"They conspired against me! The whole lot of 'em. Stole Meinhilde, my ale, and left me to do all the work." He seemed to be talking to himself, but turned to Nils. "Can you believe it?"

Nils not only could believe it, but did. But what was the best way to answer the madman? One wrong word and that knife might be in his chest next. He opened his mouth to speak, but no words were right.

The man ripped the knife from the Stitch.

Nils stammered, "I-I, uh…"

The man slid the knife on the skin of Nils' neck. "It's no matter. You're going to help me find 'em now, right?"

When Erik woke, Jonas was gone. But it was worse; he'd taken the map with him. Erik rummaged through his bag two times, then three, each time hoping the map would just appear. But it didn't. He did discover that his food was running low and he never recovered his knife from his most recent brush with death. Besides his book of fairy tales and the rope, he was left with nothing.

Nothing except...

He pulled out his stone.

He'd had this stone for six years. He never told anyone about it since that day. He and Ozzie had been playing Versteck. They'd hide a cooking pan from each other and see how long it took for the other to find it.

Dad was outside working the field. He had told them to stay inside and play. It didn't make sense then, since Erik was old enough to help and usually did. But why ask questions when you get to stay inside and play?

Erik loved playing with his little brother. Ozzie always seemed to look up to him and there were few kids around to play with anyway. But everything changed that day.

He'd heard a pounding outside. It wasn't the usual kind of noise they would hear from their father farming and Ozzie wanted to go check it out. Erik told his brother to stay inside and find the cooking pan. While Ozzie was occupied, Erik went to see what was happening.

He'd opened the front door and saw a few kids gathered around a tree. They were watching one kid throwing rocks at it. He didn't understand what kind of game it was, but he knew his father always got angry when he or Ozzie threw rocks. He ran out to them yelling. Some of the children ran away.

The boy with the rocks froze. Erik would always remember his face. He was dirty with freckles and wore a tattered shirt and no shoes. His hand hung stuck in the air, like his mom caught him in the cookie jar. The last of the kids ran off, all except him.

When Erik rounded the oak, he saw it. It wasn't the tree the boy was throwing rocks at. Suspended in the air by rope, swaying with unnatural rhythm was his father. His face was white and his neck cocked like an elbow. His face wore a pained grimace. A few stones congregated under his father's feet.

Erik's stomach collapsed and his face burned. The boy was like a statue with that same stupid expression on his face. The rest happened as if Erik were being carried by a wave. He took a stone from the ground and threw it at the boy.

It missed.

He wouldn't miss again.

He took another and ran at him. The boy dropped the stone and put his hands out in front of him, but the wave carrying Erik wouldn't stop until it crashed. He pounded the stone into the boy's chest. The boy crashed to the ground and Erik slammed down on him.

"How do you like it?" Erik yelled, smashing the stone down again and again. Tears fell from his eyes and he finally collapsed. The boy rolled away and ran off.

He would have lain there crying for hours, but Ozzie would come looking for him eventually, and he didn't want him to see their father. He stood up and pocketed the stone. He watched his father as he slumped back to the house. He cleared his eyes and whispered to himself. "It's okay. Don't let Ozzie see him. It's okay."

But from then on nothing was okay. They had to move in with Uncle Bauer and Jonas. For a while they had a room in the house, but even that didn't last long. Uncle Bauer forced them to sleep in the barn because Erik's nightmares were waking him, and everyone else, up at night.

Now Ozzie was gone too. And just like Dad, it was all his fault. He had no family left.

Not really. Even if he counted Jonas, he was gone too.

How could Jonas have done this to him? Erik settled against a tree. What could he do? He had nothing left. No friends. No brother. No map. No food. He put the stone away. He turned over his bag one last time. His broken compass fell to the ground along with the book and rope. No, still no map. He traced his finger over the rope, then grabbed it and the book and shoved them into the bag.

He pushed himself up. His legs were sore and his chest still hurt. His stomach rumbled.

Fine. Get food, then worry about what to do.

Nils flittered his fingers in the empty pouch on his belt. The crazy man took his cut of the advance, but at least he was gone. Well, for now. Nils passed over stones and leaves with no sound. He examined the landscape for movement and listened for signs of life.

Nothing yet.

He didn't doubt the crazy man was a liar, but he didn't have much of a choice. Find the children and he'll get his money back. Probably not, but he didn't even have a weapon to defend himself. Nils had two options—obey the madman or run off defenseless back to his father. Both options were dangerous, but if he stayed he might be able to get his gold back.

A shadow moved in the distant foliage. Nils leapt for cover and peered beyond. Could it be? Was he lucky enough to run into his father? That would be the best case, but better not trust to it; not in this God-forsaken forest. No, more likely it was another Stitch. And Nils had only his bare hands.

THE STITCHER

The movement was rhythmic, but vague; it sounded benign. Stitches were loud. It had to hurt them to move and break their stitching. These creatures were never meant to move like they did. Still, it was hard to pity them.

Nils could tell now the sound was walking, and on two legs. His heart beat faster and his hope was rising. He saw the outline between the trees. His stomach went numb.

It wasn't his father.

This figure was too short. Must be one of the kids, but there was still hope. Maybe the madman would honor the deal. At the very least, Nils could have a bargaining chip. It would be worth it to get his gold back.

He climbed a tree planning to ambush him from above. The boy walked toward him. The man said there were three, but he saw no evidence of anyone else. The solitary boy was wide and a cutlass hung from his side. He'd have to disable him quickly or that blade would become a problem.

Nils shifted to get in position. The branch moaned under his weight. Nils caught his breath and froze still.

The boy stopped and looked around. He peered beyond Nils, not seeming to locate the noise.

Nils exhaled slowly.

The boy walked again, but carefully. Nils had put him on alert. He needed to move another meter to be in better position, but that wasn't possible. He'd have to make do.

The boy skulked near the tree. Nils catapulted down. His elbow cracked into the boy's neck. The boy let out a quick grunt and fell to the ground. Nils' leg popped against the hard earth and he dropped also. Nils hopped up but his leg jolted with pain. A sack had dropped from the boy's grasp. From its wrapping rolled the bloody head of what looked like a fox. Its face was red with blood and there was stitching visible at the bottom. But there was something worse.

The boy was moving.

The boy growled and shot up before Nils could tackle him. "Dammit Erik, you r—" The boy's words were cut short when they locked eyes. "Who're you?" he said, cracking his neck and withdrawing the cutlass.

The boy's eyes were red and watery. His neck no doubt hurt badly, but without a weapon this fight wouldn't be in Nils' favor. He backed away, swiveled, and ran. His leg collapsed in pain and he tumbled to the rocks.

"Yer not going anywhere. You gotta pay for what you did," The boy said.

Nils flipped over and crossed his arms. The boy loomed over him with the sword raised. His eyes were wide. His crazed face looked familiar. It was just like the madman's. He must be his son. "Stop! I know where you father is."

The boy hesitated. His brow furrowed and his arm wobbled in the air. He stepped back and lowered the sword. "What're you talking about?"

"He ambushed me out here looking for you," Nils said, standing up. "He took my money and gear and told me I could get it back by finding you."

The boy scratched his chest. "So yer plan was to knock me out and hand me over?" The boy's face hardened. He strode forward and kicked Nils to the ground. "Who are you anyway? And what're you doing in Odenwald?"

"Look, I'm not your enemy," Nils stammered. "I'm sorry I attacked you. Your dad left me defenseless out here. He took my gun and sword. This forest isn't safe without a weapon."

The boy rubbed his neck, staring at Nils. "You mean because of the Stitches?"

"Exactly, but it looks like you've already had a run-in with them."

"What the hell're you doing here anyway?"

Nils pushed himself up. "I'm trying to rescue a girl from Erbach."

"It looks like yer the one needing rescuing now." The boy laughed. "If yer smart, you'll follow my lead and get out of here."

He'd love to leave this place, but that wasn't an option. Not without Pia, and not without his father. "You know your father is looking for you and your friends? And I think he's gone beyond just wanting to discipline you."

The boy put his sword away and picked up the fox head. "He's just sore because I took his ale. But when I find him, he'll be happy to see me. It's the other two he hates."

That couldn't be true, but Nils wasn't about to argue about it. "Good luck. I'm Nils by the way."

"Jonas." He sauntered away.

"Where are you going?"

"Open yer ears. I'm going home."

"Can't you help me?"

"No," Jonas said, striding off.

Nils limped after him. The pain would subside soon, but he couldn't let Jonas leave him defenseless. "Please. I'll help you."

Jonas stopped, dropped the sacked head, and rubbed his shoulder.

"I can carry that head for you," Nils said.

"Why'd you wanna do that?"

"It's dangerous out here. I don't wanna get killed."

Jonas kicked the head. It rolled toward Nils. "Fine, carry the head and you can follow me. One false move though and yer dead."

Erik cursed the fish. He tried catching them with a sharpened stick, but they escaped his stabs. His stomach was tight. It was either worry for Ozzie or hunger, but he would need to eat either way. Unfortunately, the fish proved too difficult to capture.

He walked along the river watching their shadows move through the water. The rushes flowed into a hole in a rock along the side of the bank. Fish ended up getting trapped in the tiny cave and wriggling out after some difficulty. It was the perfect natural trap. Erik drew near the cove and flung his hands into the hole, trapping a fish against the wall.

He pulled the fish out, careful not to let it slip between his hands and the wall. He slammed it against a rock on the shore and threw it to the side. He thrust his hands into the trap again. He pinned another fish to the wall.

Too bad for the fish. He could've pinned any other, but this was the one he caught. That was just the way of life though. He beat the fish into the rock and tossed it to the side.

Another fish floated into the trap. It wriggled as it tried to swim past the jutted rock wall. It splashed out of the water briefly and its body thrashed until it finally escaped the confines and swam back into the main stream of the river.

Escape was possible.

He turned to the two dead fish and considered their eyes. They were open just as it if they were alive. "I know it's not fair," he muttered. "But I know how you feel."

Odenwald wasn't the road he thought it was; it was a trap. Yes, and they were the fish, both him and his brother. The only question left was if they could still wriggle out of this mess. Maybe he could, but what about Ozzie?

Was there still time?

Erik took the fish and scraped it against a rock, doing his best to remove its scales. Why didn't Ozzie listen to him? He wouldn't have been in this situation if he had just followed orders. Stay hidden. Erik flayed the fish against the rock harder. It was easier for him to blame Ozzie, but he knew he was just trying to ignore the truth: he brought him here. It was his fault.

He forced a stick through each fish, built a fire, and suspended them over the flames to cook. The fire was small. Hopefully small enough to evade detection. But even if it wasn't, what could he do? Maybe he deserved to be killed anyway.

The smoke rose into the trees. On a branch high above sat a familiar figure. The owl was back, watching him. Blood rushed to Erik's face and his nose tingled with heat. He fists clenched. "What do you want from me?"

The owl didn't move. Erik's chest heaved with a quickened heartbeat. He didn't know what to make of the bird, but he was tired of being watched. He breathed deep the smell of roasting fish. They darkened in the heat. He wished Ozzie was there to eat with him. A branch cracked above. The owl was gone. Where'd it go?

Wind tickled his hair as the owl swooped by and grabbed a fish with its talons. It flew into the woods and perched.

Erik rose to his feet and his face hardened. He was sick of all the games. Did the owl want him to follow again? It may have brought him to the river, but it stood perched deeper into the forest.

Weaponless, deeper into the forest? Without a map, deeper into the forest. No, he would not go farther into the trap. His only option was to follow the river back and hope to break away at the right spot to get back to Steinau. If he was lucky, maybe he'd even find Jonas. "Sorry, bird, not this time."

After an hour, Nils' leg felt much better, but now his left shoulder pounded with pain. He never realized how heavy a head could be. He flung the bloodied package over his right shoulder and followed Jonas.

"Why would you keep this thing anyway?" Nils asked.

Jonas just shook his head and continued walking.

"Are you a hunter? Is it some kind of trophy?"

Jonas took a flask from his pocket and took a drink. He put it away, wiped his mouth with his arm, and coughed. Obviously he didn't want to talk about it. But Nils was still curious. What was Jonas doing out here? And where were his friends?

"It must've been hard to kill this thing all by yourself," Nils said. "But I guess you had your friends to help you."

Jonas' steps slowed. "You don't know what yer talking about."

Nils smiled. He got a reaction. "Actually, I know exactly what I'm talking about. When my father and I were attacked by one of those things, it took both of us to take it down. They're relentless."

Jonas swooshed around. He lumbered forward and pointed at the head. "I killed that bastard all on my own!" His face was red. "In fact I saved Erik's life. That thing was tearing him to shreds." He turned and marched forward. "So excuse me if I wanted a keepsake."

"Sorry I asked," Nils said. Hot tempers must run in the family. They walked for a minute in silence. "By the way, who's Erik? One of your friends?"

Jonas scoffed. "He's the idiot who brought us here."

That would make Jonas the idiot who followed him. Nils dared not say it though. He was in no position to point out Jonas' stupidity. "Why'd he do that? Didn't he know how dangerous it was here?"

"We heard stories. We just didn't believe them."

"But why'd you all leave in the first place?"

"They had their reasons, I had mine."

"Like what?" Nils asked.

"Mind yer own business," Jonas said.

He was a tough nut to crack, but Nils needed more than just safety. He needed information.

"Where are they now? The other two you came here with?"

Jonas stopped and looked at Nils. "Why d'ya wanna know that?" His eyes narrowed on him. "You wanna find them for my father, like you tried to cash me in?" Jonas shook his head. "He's not gonna give you any of your stuff back, so don't even try."

"I'm not trying to cash anybody in. At this point, I just need to find my father. I'd go alone, but not without my rifle. If you can get me that, I'll be happy to leave you all alone."

"Sorry, but I can't get you anything. My Dad ain't giving you anything back, either, even if you get him Erik and Ozzie."

Was Jonas trying to protect them? "If you care so much about them, why aren't you with them right now?"

Jonas turned and resumed walking, his back to Nils. "The only one I care about right now is myself. Erik wanted me to help him get his brother back from the Stitch that took him. But it's suicide." Jonas sighed and scratched his chest. "I'm not trying to save them from you or my father. They're in deeper trouble than that, and I don't want any part of it."

One of them got taken? If Jonas knew where, it would make Nils' search for the Stitcher a lot easier. "Do you know where it took him?"

"I didn't stick around to find out. It's their problem, not mine."

"You just left them?"

"What about you?" Jonas said, turning around. His fists were clenched and his teeth gnashed at Nils. "Did you leave your father or did he leave you? When it comes down to life and death, everybody's gonna look after their own ass. Yer no better than me! You tried to knock me out to save yerself."

Nils felt the hot rush of blood through his veins. "My father and I split up to track your father. The only reason we're not together right now is because your dad's a maniac and tied me up." Nils took in a heavy breath. "My father would never leave me."

"My father only woulda tied you up if you were doing something stupid. You probably shoved your gun in his face or something," Jonas said. "Anyway, I'm getting tired of yer stupid questions. Either shut yer mouth or go off and die."

Nils'd gone over the line, but Jonas didn't have much useful information anyway. He'd just have to shut up and bide his time.

FALLEN FRUIT

Erik jogged.

The rushing of the water could do nothing to distract his mind. He was abandoning his brother, like Dad had abandoned him.

Wings fluttered behind him. The owl was still following him. Erik sped up, but it was impossible to outrun the bird. What did it want from him? "Just leave me alone already," Erik said.

It didn't answer.

"What do you want me to do?" Erik asked.

The only sounds were the pounding of Erik's own feet and the swooshing of wings behind him.

He guessed that the bird wanted him to follow it, but he couldn't go farther into the forest. Jonas was right. He *did* need his help surviving in Odenwald. So did Ozzie. "If you're really trying to help me, find Ozzie."

The owl didn't answer. The wind whistled in the branches, but there was something else too. Footsteps? Erik stopped and held his breath. No, maybe it was just his imagination.

THUD!

Erik groaned. A branch had banged him on the shoulder. He crouched and rubbed it.

The owl hovered over him, and retreated. "What the hell's your problem?" Erik asked. This forest had driven him crazy. He was talking to birds now? "Never mind, forget it."

"Never mind, what?"

Erik jolted. The voice wasn't from the owl; it echoed from the opposite direction. Uncle Bauer emerged from behind a tree, his rifle aimed at Erik. His hair was dirty and his body was covered in dry sweat. Uncle Bauer's hands shook, but Erik didn't like the way he was pointing the rifle at him.

"You again? Where's Jonas?" Uncle Bauer asked.

Erik wasn't going to wait another second with a gun pointed at him. He dashed for the cover of the woods.

"Where d'ya think yer going?"

BANG!

The shot echoed off the trees. Erik tumbled to the ground and rolled on the rocks behind an oak. He patted down his body. Everything looked fine, but the sound of Uncle Bauer trampling and breathing was getting closer, along with something else he couldn't discern.

He dashed into a densely wooded area away from the river. "Why are you trying to kill me?" Erik yelled out as he retreated. He crawled behind a small rock cliff and silenced his breathing.

"Where's Jonas?" Uncle Bauer's roar was closer than Erik expected.

He peered over the top of the rock cliff. Uncle Bauer's boots stomped directly in front of him. Erik startled and Uncle Bauer seized his shoulders, lifted him over the rock, and tossed him over his side. Erik cracked on the earth. His chest stabbed with pain.

Uncle Bauer picked his gun up and cocked it. "Last chance, rat. Where's Jonas?"

Unfortunately, he didn't know. But that wouldn't satisfy Uncle Bauer. "He's...I uh...he went...um..." His mind flooded with thoughts of the last couple days.

"Stop stuttering ya worthless dog. Yer as pathetic as he is!" Uncle Bauer raised the rifle. Erik scrambled back and tensed.

"What the h—" Uncle Bauer swiveled.

BANG!

Uncle Bauer yelled.

A snake had its teeth sunk into Uncle Bauer's wrist and his rifle dropped to the ground. But that snake was just the tail of a larger Stitch. It had an wild boar's body, but with a goat's head. A long tusk protruding from its neck, which it swung at Uncle

Bauer's legs. It punctured him and he toppled to the ground and grabbed his rifle. The snake rushed at his neck and sunk its fangs deep into his flesh. He jerked back and arched on the ground. He released the gun, seized the snake, and with a quick clench, cracked it like a peanut shell.

Erik raced away from the battle. He wasn't about to sit around and wait to see who would win. Whatever the outcome, the victor would get him next. It wasn't a time for hide and seek either, so he would sprint until his legs or lungs gave up, and then run some more.

It wasn't long before he bent over in exhaustion. His legs screamed at him and he coughed as he inhaled. His stomach ached and he felt queasy. Still, he needed to catch his breath so he could listen. He swallowed a deep breath.

Someone was arguing, and not far off. It wasn't Uncle Bauer, and it wasn't a Stitch. He choked out his breath and limped toward the sound.

After a minute of wheezing and pain he saw someone. He looked about the same age as himself, only his clothes were nicer. His hair was short and blond and he stood a little shorter than Erik. He'd never seen him before, but he was carrying a sack that he had seen before. It was Jonas' trophy.

"Erik, is it?" the boy asked.

How'd he know his name? Who was this and why was he carrying the head of the Stitch Jonas killed? Unfortunately, there was no time for answers.

"Do you have a weapon? A rifle, or a knife, or something?" Erik asked.

The boy shrugged and shook his head.

"I'm being chased and I can't just stand here and chat. Can you help me?"

The boy peered beyond him. "Who's chasing you?"

"I'm not sure right now. It depends on who kills who."

The boy's eyes widened. "You *are* Erik, right?"

"Yes, what does that matter?"

"Come with me, I know where to go."

Erik trailed the boy who identified himself as Nils, but tripped to the ground panting for breath. He sprawled on the ground, but it felt like he was falling into the earth.

"Just lie down here, I'll be right back," Nils told him.

Erik pushed himself up against a fallen tree and rested his head in his hands. His chest burned and his legs were stiff. He tried to take long breaths, but coughed when inhaling.

After a moment, Nils returned. Jonas was with him.

Erik jumped to his feet and darted at Jonas. "You left me alone to die, ya thief!"

Jonas grabbed Erik's throat and threw him to the ground. "You never wanted me around anyway, so stop whining about it."

Erik crashed to the ground. He couldn't beat Jonas, least of all when every part of his body was spent.

"He said someone was chasing him," Nils said.

"My dad?" Jonas asked. "Did you see him?"

Erik struggled to his feet. "Last time I saw him he was fighting off a Stitch, but it doesn't matter which one wins. Either one will be coming to kill me next."

Jonas grabbed Erik by his jacket and pulled him close. Erik could smell ale on Jonas' breath. He turned away. "What do you mean it doesn't matter which one wins? Do you want my dad to die?"

Erik jabbed Jonas' side. Jonas grunted and dropped Erik.

"You little filth," Jonas said and punched him in the stomach.

Erik collapsed and coughed into the dirt.

"Shouldn't we be getting out of here?" Nils asked.

Jonas' eyes were wide and his hand was on the hilt of his sword. "I gotta help my dad," he said. "C'mon! And don't leave the head, either."

Jonas ran off. Nils hesitated, but followed him.

Erik wiped the sweat from his face. He didn't have time to rest, but he rolled under a rock and closed his eyes. He just needed a minute.

When Ozzie opened his eyes he was in a cage. The room was dark. The windows were boarded over.

The air was thick with blood and rotting flesh. Ozzie shook his head and saw a stump where his right arm used to be. It was stitched and bandaged. The realization of a dull stabbing pain became pronounced. He clenched his teeth and moaned, then whimpered.

A shadow moved in a cage across the room. It was very dark, but it looked like a girl. Her hair was long and brown and her complexion corpselike in color. She must've been here a long time. She had blindfolds over her eyes that were stitched onto her skin. She held her neck.

She whispered, "Is someone here?"

Ozzie whispered back, "Yeah. I'm Ozzie. Who're you?"

"Oh. I've never heard of you before. I'm not supposed to talk to you."

That was strange. What was she afraid of? Ozzie's eyes adjusted to the darkness. Parts of animals, legs, torsos, even heads, were stacked in piles and strewn about the room. There were bloody cloths bunched up and laying haphazardly around the floor and on chairs. A large wooden table upheld knives of all sizes and something familiar. He could taste the vomit rising in his throat. It was his own severed right arm.

"Where am I?" Ozzie asked.

"This's where he works on the Meat."

"Who?"

"The Stitcher."

"What? And he works on…meat?"

"That's what all this is called, you and me too."

The stump that used to be his arm felt wet. Flies buzzed near a pile of limbs and inside the sockets of a deer's head. There were knife marks around the sockets. Maybe the girl was lucky she was unable to see all this. The Stitcher must've cut her eyes out too.

"We have to get out of here," Ozzie said.

"It's no use," she said. "It's impossible."

"Well, we have to try."

"It'll be better for you if you don't," she said. "Besides, I've tried."

"What happened?"

"He caught me and brought me back. After that he lowered the pain-killers."

"Has anyone ever escaped?"

She shook her head. "How would I know? I can't see."

"Well, there's gotta be a way out," Ozzie said.

"Even if there is, it's no use, he's p—"

A creaking came from wooden stairs outside the room.

"He's what?" Ozzie asked.

The door swung open and a tall man walked toward Ozzie. He was thin and somber with a clean shaven face. He wore thick glasses. His grey eyes magnified large on his head, like an owl. He withdrew a key from his breast pocket. His fingers looked unusually long and slender. He unlocked the cage and grabbed Ozzie by the throat.

He kicked and grunted but the man jabbed into Ozzie's arm nub. Ozzie yelped and his eyes broke forth with tears. It felt like a knife had just dug between his bones.

"Don't struggle or I'll make it worse," he said. His voice was calm and slow.

Ozzie sniffled and tightened his throat. The girl was right about one thing: struggling made it worse.

"That's a good boy," the man said. "You should be thanking me; your arm was getting very bad. The infection would've killed you if I hadn't removed it."

He throttled Ozzie against the wooden table and examined his stitching. "It looks like you're going to live after all."

The man's eyes were busy, looking over Ozzie's body. With his thick glasses, his huge eyes darted and twitched like insect legs, but then they became very still, and Ozzie very uncomfortable. The man glared into Ozzie's eyes.

Ozzie turned his head, but the man choked him. "Look at me," he said. "Don't move."

Ozzie obeyed.

The man relaxed his grip, squinted his eyes, and shook his head.

"What do you want from me?" Ozzie stammered.

He lifted Ozzie up. "Unfortunately, you're the wrong one."

He shoved Ozzie back in his cage and locked it. He returned the key to his pocket and looked at Ozzie. "But I know you didn't come alone. I have another use for you."

This was Jonas' chance. His father needed him. His dad had taken so many hunting trips into the forest with Krause and never once did he take him. And the night of the harvest changed everything. Seeing Krause that night, with Jonas' own gun, he knew his father didn't respect him for shit. Four years Jonas'd worked for that rifle. Four wasted years.

But now he'd be able to show his father his strength. His dad would learn that Jonas wasn't just another rat. He wasn't just some dog. Meinhilde felt heavy and dangerous in his hands. He liked it.

Jonas shouted, "Dad! Where are you?"

Labored breathing pervaded the forest.

Jonas whispered to Nils, "stay behind me."

They crept toward the heavy breathing. His father was nowhere in sight but there was a boulder and trees before them. Nothing was in the branches.

Nils whispered, "I think he's behind the rock."

Jonas peered behind the boulder. He shot back and crashed into Nils. "Look out! It's a Stitch."

But it didn't move. It just stared at them. It had a goat's head, and a tusk protruded from its neck on both sides. Its body was large and furry, but dark red and wet with blood. Stitched to it was not quite a tail, but a whole snake, the head of which had been crushed.

"Looks like this one's done for," Nils said. "Should we find your father?"

Jonas inched closer to the Stitch. Its eyes followed him as he approached. Its skin was tearing around its tusk. "It looks like it was put here for attacking, but it's cutting through its neck."

"That's what the Stitcher does," Nils said.

Jonas took hold of the tusk. "The Stitcher?" He tore the tusk out. The creature flailed, unable to breathe. It fell still, dead. "Who's the Stitcher?"

"Are you kidding? You don't know? He's the one who makes these monsters," Nils said.

Jonas straightened and threw the tusk to the ground. "Yeah, but why?"

"No one really knows," Nils said, "'cept him."

Jonas wiped his bloody hand into the dirt, and dusted his hands. "I don't think I really want to know why. C'mon, let's go find my dad."

"Look," Nils said, pointing to the ground. "There're splotches of blood on the ground. The snake head must've left a trail."

"Let's go."

Jonas spotted the blood easily on the dirt and rocks, but the grassy terrain proved more difficult. He called for his father.

His father groaned in the distance.

Jonas ran toward the sound. Meinhilde loosened in his grasp when he saw his father.

He sat slumped against a tree, covered in vomit and blood. His neck and face were swollen and white. He gagged on shallow breaths. His right leg revealed several bleeding punctures. The battle must've been brutal. He'd never seen his father so pale. Jonas' hands quaked. He rushed to his father. Nils shadowed him.

"D-Dad, can y-you hear me?" Jonas asked.

His father's head inched up, but he didn't look at him. "You little shit." He grabbed Jonas' arm, but his grasp was weak. His ballooned neck had two punctures. He must've been bitten by that viper.

"Are you o-o-okay?"

His father's hand released Jonas and dropped to the ground. "This's all your goddam' fault," he said, coughing.

Jonas shook his head. "N-no. You don't un-understand."

His father convulsed and clasped his chest. His hands trembled and his face contorted.

"Get up and move away," Nils said.

Nils pointed a rifle at Jonas.

"What the hell are you doing?" Jonas asked.

"Take the gold on his belt and throw it to me," Nils said. His eyes were fixed on Jonas. Nils stepped closer, gun steady in his grasp.

"My father's dying! Help me."

Nils shook his head. "I'm sorry, but I need my gold back. Just pick it up and throw it to me and you'll never see me again."

Jonas' father was still. No more convulsions. His hands lay in the dirt. Jonas couldn't believe it. It couldn't be real. His father wasn't ever supposed to die. His throat tightened and tears welled in his eyes.

He grabbed the pouch and squeezed it. He clenched his jaw and launched it at Nils.

Nils sidestepped. The pouch flew past him. Rifle locked on Jonas, Nils backed up, knelt down and retrieved the pouch from the ground. "For what it's worth, it's not your fault."

Jonas clenched his fists. Who the hell did he think he was? He didn't know a goddam thing about Jonas, or his father. "Don't you ever speak to me again."

"I'm sorry," Nils said, disappearing into the forest.

It never should've happened like this. Jonas knelt down by his father and rested his hand on his chest. There was no heartbeat. He didn't even have a chance to save him. He never got to prove his worth, and he never would.

His father's words echoed in his mind. He was wrong, though. It wasn't Jonas' fault. That was the only thing Nils was right about. It wasn't his fault at all. None of this ever would've happened if it hadn't been for Erik and his idiot brother, and he meant to make that fact known.

The rock was still in the blue tree. Erik knew it was immovable, but he felt an unstoppable urge to remove it. When he stretched forth his hand to take the stone from the center of the tree the ground crumbled beneath him.

He plummeted down and was caught by the neck in the roots of the tree. He wriggled against the roots, but they constricted all the more and his breathing became thin. He stopped struggling and the roots loosened. He couldn't escape, but at least he could breath.

Erik noticed a man in front of him, caught up in the roots by the neck also. Déjà vu. He had the white cover over his head, except now there were three figures. Each one hung silently with white sheets on their heads. They were all dead, just like he would be.

Erik reached and took hold of the cloth over one man's head. When he pulled it off, the face of his father stared back at him, white and motionless. His frown made him look disappointed, even angry.

Erik moved to replace the white sheet when his father's mouth moved.

"It's your fault."

Nils crept through the forest. He wanted to get to the glade quickly, but there was no point in being careless. Running may get him there faster, but it also made more noise. He had his gun back, but Stitches were too dangerous, even for an armed hunter.

He stepped over rocks and around bushes when something red and white in the dirt captured his attention. He knelt down and took it in his hand. It was a doll. Dirty and missing an arm, with a red and white checkered dress. It had small button-eyes. Well, at least one; the other was missing.

The stories he'd heard of the Stitcher were that he took children, only children. He turned the doll over, feeling its soft texture. He didn't know if it belonged to someone the Stitcher captured, but he thought of Pia. He needed to find her alive. Missing an arm or eye would be okay, but dead would do him no good.

Pia was a young girl taken from her parents in the night, a story Nils and his father had heard many times before they came to the forest. It always started with unusual birds. Some claimed they had eyes all over their bodies, but few saw them up close. After that, they all reported a similar experience; a beast of some kind would break into the house and carry the child away. Anyone who tried to stop it would be killed or wounded.

But Pia's parents didn't just have a story to tell, they also had money, and money speaks a language like nothing else. But even hunters weren't brave enough to take up arms to go into Odenwald, even for a windfall. Nils knew he wasn't brave enough, and his father wasn't a great hunter either, but they had other reasons.

He dropped the doll to the ground and checked his pouch of gold again to make sure it was all accounted for. It was the only thing that was going to make this descent into hell worth the pain.

He resumed his journey toward the glade, but the quiet in the air reminded him that there may be nothing when he got there. His father couldn't wait for him forever. He probably left to search for him, but hopefully he left a note, or something to let him know where he was.

It wouldn't be long now. He knew he shouldn't let it, but his heart grew in anticipation to either see or hear from his father.

"It's your fault," Jonas said and stomped Erik's stomach.

Erik woke with a cough and covered his stomach. Jonas' face was hot and he could feel tears dripping down his cheeks, but he didn't care if Erik saw him cry. He wanted him to know how bad the pain was.

"He's dead," Jonas said. "And you left him there." He seized Erik by the neck, pulled him up and punched his face.

Erik collapsed on the ground, holding a hand to his cheek. "Stop. I couldn't help him, he was shooting at me."

Jonas took a step back and took out Meinhilde. "Look at me," he said.

Erik lowered his arms. Jonas' chest heaved with each breath. His hands were bloody and the light smell of vomit reminded him of his father.

"All of this is because of you," Jonas said. "I never should've followed you." He slid Meinhilde under Erik's throat. Jonas' grip tightened around the hilt. Pain pulsed in his hand.

Erik's body straightened. His neck and arms tensed. His eyes closed and he reached into his pocket.

It was like clockwork. He'd seen Erik shove his hand into his pocket for years and never thought much about it. But now he would know. "What the hell's in your damned pocket?" Jonas asked. "Take it out, now!"

Erik's eyes opened. He hesitated a second, but withdrew his hand, along with a rock.

He wouldn't have guessed it in a million years. "A rock?" he asked. "What kind of idiot are you? Why are you carrying a rock around?"

Erik shook his head and his eyes avoided Jonas. "Talk ya rat."

Erik's eyes rose to Jonas. "This rock is the last memory I have of my father. When he hanged himself, these kids were throwing stones at him from the road. And I...uh..."

Erik choked and tears precipitated in his eyes. Jonas pulled Meinhilde back an inch.

Erik continued, "I picked one up from under his body and I…I, um…bashed it into some kid."

Jonas was surprised. As far as he knew, Erik only fought when he was sticking up for Ozzie.

"What happened?" Jonas asked.

"I tackled him and beat his chest again and again with the rock."

"Did you kill him?"

Erik shook his head. "I wanted to, but I stopped."

"Why?"

"I was so angry, but I realized it wasn't his fault. It was mine. It all hit me at once. I was angry at my dad for killing himself but I was angrier at myself for not being good enough. If I'd been better, he wouldn't have done it." Tears streamed down Erik's face. "Because of me, Ozzie lost his dad, and now because of me, he's dead too."

Jonas lowered the sword and sat down across from Erik. It was like looking into a mirror. Jonas was never a good enough son either. Well, he *was*, but Dad'd never given him the chance to prove it. He withdrew a bottle he'd stolen and rolled it from hand to hand.

"Did it feel good to beat up that kid?" Jonas asked.

Erik shook his head and put his rock back into his pocket. He wiped the tears from his face.

"Why do you still carry the rock around?" Jonas asked.

"I don't really know," Erik said. "It's just a part of me now. It helps me deal with the pain."

Jonas shook the bottle of ale, listening to the splashing. "You and Ozzie think I'm just like him, don't you?" Jonas asked.

Erik palmed his bruised cheek and looked down, clearing his throat. "Well, you've got his sword, his ale, and you've been carrying around a Stitch head lately."

He was half right. He'd left the head when Nils went renegade, but he did still have Meinhilde and the ale. He shook his head. "He shouldn't be dead. Now he'll never know."

"Never know what?"

"That I'm not worthless."

Erik nodded. "You saved my life. That's more than I could ever say for him."

Jonas unscrewed the bottle and lifted it to his mouth, letting the aroma rise in his nostrils. "I just wanted to go hunting with him." He lowered the ale. "I'm not trying to be just like him."

"You're not *just* like him. You only tried to kill me once, he did it twice."

Jonas smirked. "I don't think I could actually kill another person." He stood up and flung the bottle into a rock, shattering it.

Erik stood up, too. "What d'we do now?"

"I'm going home. What about you?"

"I need to find Ozzie," Erik said. "But it's impossible…"

Jonas nodded. There was nothing he could do to help. Ozzie was gone. Probably dead. And it wasn't worth his life tracking down a ghost. "I'm sorry," he said and walked. To Jonas' surprise, Erik followed him. Erik must've lost hope too.

THE HANGING MAN

The thin scent of blood lingered in the air. Vultures cawed above him. Nils feared the worst, but hoped it was just a dead animal.

It wasn't.

A tree stood the other side of a pond. Suspended from one of its branches was a man. Nils sprinted through the pond, half-swimming until he reached the dry ground. Heat pressed in his nose. There was no longer any doubt. It was him. Blood dripped from his father's leg into a dark red pool beneath him.

Against the base of the tree Nils found his father's belongings, including a note.

Nils,

We came to right place. The Stitcher is near.

The reports are true.

Get out of the forest.

If you find me, I'm sorry.

Dad

Nils blew out a sigh. His strength drained out of him and his head sunk. Scattered on the ground were the gold coins his father had carried with him.

There was still a job to do.

He picked up the coins and put them away. His father's face was pale. His expression seemed sad, as if he somehow knew his final wish would not be honored.

Nils' throat felt blocked and his breaths were shallow. He knew he should cry, but it just wasn't coming. At the foot of the tree were his father's weapons, a couple swords and some knives. He took a knife and a sword. There was no need for more, they'd only weigh him down. He also gathered the newspaper articles. Most featured stories about missing children, but one was about his mother.

No, he couldn't leave Odenwald now. There was too much riding on the mission. His father had only warned him to leave because he loved him, but it was never about them. It was about Mom. Nils was sure that if the situation were reversed, his father would do the same thing. The only thing that mattered was getting Pia back. Then came the payment, then he could save Mom.

Erik walked. Each step he took felt like a betrayal. Ozzie would never have left him for dead, but then again, Ozzie probably *was* dead. Jonas was right when he'd kicked Erik in the stomach; this was all his fault. He'd only been trying to protect Ozzie, but it all went wrong. Just like his plan to get back at Jonas with the forged letter. The wrong person got hurt. Ozzie never deserved any of this. It should've been him, not Ozzie.

"Did you say something?" Jonas asked.

Erik snapped back to reality. "What? No. Sorry, I was just daydreaming."

"I thought I heard something. Hurry up. I don't want to spend another minute in this forest."

Erik nodded and trailed Jonas. What would they do when they got home anyway? Just run the farm without Uncle Bauer? He didn't really do much work anyway. But still, without Ozzie, it just didn't feel right.

A crash exploded behind them. It sounded like a tree had been split in two.

Before he could turn, Erik shot forward face-first to the ground. He pushed to roll over, but the weight on his back was too great. A roar bellowed from behind him and he grasped about for a rock, a stick, or anything, but all he got was dirt and weeds. Sharp pain sliced into his side. A scream erupted out of his mouth. The maw of the creature enveloped him.

Jonas unsheathed Meinhilde and dashed to Erik. He slashed into the Stitch's neck. It roared, releasing Erik, and he tumbled to the ground. Erik grunted and held his side. Blood dripped between his fingers.

The creature had a boar's head with tusks, an elk's body, and a fat, long tail. Its eyes were wide like full moons. It crashed toward Jonas. Jonas swung at the monster's neck again, but it recoiled and whipped its tail, swiping him to the ground. Jonas hit the ground but bounced back up.

Erik leapt to his feet as well. Daggers of pain pierced his side. "I'll distract him," he yelled to Jonas, staggering to the back of the creature.

The Stitch turned to Erik and stomped close. Jonas charged and stabbed its tail. Its head flew upwards letting out a screech. Jonas withdrew his sword and swung at its neck, but the blow never landed. Its tail slammed into him. Jonas tumbled to the ground, dropping Meinhilde. The Stitch loomed over Jonas and crushed his chest with its hoof. Erik rushed at the monster hitting it with his fists.

Jonas choked. His face whitened and his eyes were frantic.

"Get off of him!" Erik screamed, pounding the Stitch. Its skin was hard like a wall, and Erik's blows were just as useless as hitting one.

Jonas lay motionless; his face void of all expression. The Stitch charged Erik to the ground. It inched toward him, mouth open. Erik scrambled with his legs, crawling back against a rock. He was pinned. The Stitch pounced at him, but an owl swooshed in and scraped its eye with its talons. It staggered back, thrashing its tusks in the air. The owl perched on a tree, then flew into the forest. Erik rose to his feet and raced after it.

He hit sprinting speed when he was tackled to the ground by the Stitch. Erik cried out. The owl turned and flew back, but it was too far to help now. He flipped over. The monster loomed over him. He'd survived many brushes with death in Odenwald, but he resigned that his number was up. Its teeth, sharp and glazed with saliva, drove forward toward his throat. Erik tensed. The flutter of wings were still too distant.

The Stitch's mouth brushed against Erik's neck, but it let out a scream, its body flailing away from him.

Jonas' words came like a choked whisper. "Hurry up! Get out of here!" His face was still white, but his eyes had life. He pulled Meinhilde from the creature's back and thrust it through its leg with a sawing motion. The creature toppled and screamed into the air. Jonas flashed an angry look at Erik. "Go already!"

Erik jumped to his feet and located the owl, which had perched. It took flight the moment Erik saw it. He knew what to do. He sprinted after the bird.

Erik looked back to see how Jonas fared. He thrust Meinhilde at the Stitch's head, but the creature snapped its jaw around Jonas' neck. With a quick crack, it tossed his body to the side. It turned toward Erik and galloped, but its leg buckled like a broken twig. It crashed to the ground, screaming and writhing on the ground, unable to carry its own weight.

Erik turned, anchored his watery gaze on the owl, and ran.

Thud. Thud. Thud. Erik's feet pounded the ground in a steady pace.

His body was pain. His legs were fire. His lungs inhaled air like ice, but he didn't care. Every pain was but a whisper compared to Jonas' accusation echoing in his mind. *It's all your fault.* He was right; it was. First Ozzie, then Uncle Bauer, now Jonas. He'd brought everyone to their doom, and yet he himself survived. He'd hated Jonas, who saved him twice from the Stitches. And what was Jonas' reward? He watched his father die, only to die himself the same day. And all for what?

Thud. Thud. Thud.

The owl flew ahead of him. Where were they going? Why'd it guide him? What made him so special? It didn't really matter. There was no getting out alive. If Jonas and Uncle Bauer couldn't survive, there was no hope for Erik. He never thought he'd admire Jonas. And now he was dead, too. He grabbed at the rock in his pocket. What was Jonas' sacrifice all for? Just to save Erik? What a waste.

The owl perched on a tree in the distance. The shadows were long in the forest and the air was cool in Erik's lungs, but tainted with a putrid smell. The stars would be glimmering in the sky soon. He slowed his jog to a walk, continuing his rhythmic breathing until his heartbeat slowed. Why'd the owl stop? Was it time for a rest? Or was there something important about this place?

He approached the tree. Under the owl hung a rope, and from that rope hung a man. Erik turned away and gasped, falling to a squat. He shook his head. What kind of perverse joke was this? The smell of old blood invaded his nostrils. He inched back up and approached the body.

Blood pooled under his body from the man's wounded leg. He'd tied a tourniquet around it. His face was grey and his head tilted in that nauseating bend he'd first seen on his father. Why was he brought here?

It must've been Odenwald's final black joke at his expense. The forest was cursed, and now so was he. He collapsed to the ground and watched the hanging man sway in the wind. Could anything come to this forest and not die? He grabbed his stone. He never should've forced Ozzie to leave.

It was all his fault.

The hanging man blurred in Erik's vision. Maybe that was his destiny too. Everyone else had died. Now it was his turn. Above him, still perched, was the silhouette of the owl. He'd thought that even through it all, at least the weird bird was on his side. But it was just another cruel trick. No, there was nothing left, except to be killed by one of those Stitches.

But he had a better idea.

Erik opened his bag. There was his book and the rope. He nodded and removed the rope. It would be better than being killed by a Stitch. He tied it into a noose and climbed the tree. He chose a different branch from the hanging man. He didn't want the branch to break from too much weight. He tied the other end of the rope around the branch and slid the noose around his neck.

He closed his eyes and took a deep breath.

He sat a moment, grinding his teeth. His face was tense. Was this how his father felt before he hanged himself? He exhaled and relaxed his muscles.

He couldn't do it.

He opened his eyes. His arms quivered. Where was his courage? He dug his hand into his pocket and squeezed his rock until pain submerged his mind. This was his last chance to show Odenwald that it couldn't kill him. No Stitch would get the chance. He was the one to blame for all of this anyway. He should be the one to do it.

He released the rock and slipped his leg off the branch, letting gravity pull his body down. His body jerked as the rope snapped around his neck. His eyes widened and he gagged, trying to inhale. He seized the rope, instinctively pulling against it, but it only tightened. He kicked violently, suspended over the grass and dirt. Did his father experience the same panic?

Was he losing his mind?

The ground accelerated toward him. His leg cracked against the earth, followed by a jolt to his head. He sat up, wheezing. He loosened the rope and looked up. It'd snapped.

"Be not overly wicked, neither be a fool," a voice said. "Why should you die before your time?"

Mere meters from Erik stood the owl. Only, it wasn't a normal owl. Krause was right. It had multiple eyes sewn into its body, and instead of a beak, it had the face of a small monkey. Erik jumped back. "Holy shit! W-what are you?"

"What I am is a Stitch, but who I am is more important."

Erik shook his head and nearly fainted. His neck burned and he held it, which only hurt more. "But," Erik said, "animals can't talk."

The Stitch spread its wings and hobbled forward. "That's true. But I'm not just an animal; I'm a Stitch. That means I used to be human, like you," he said. "And please, call me Vergis."

The Stitch's eyes watched Erik's face intelligently, but it was still hard to believe. *It* used to be human? Was this a hallucination? There were so many questions. Who made it? Why had it been following him? But he'd have to settle for one at a time.

"Why'd you cut my rope?"

Vergis' eyes shifted left and he cleared his throat. "Why should a fool have a price in his hand to buy wisdom, when he has no mind?"

Erik scratched his head. "What are you talking about?"

"It means you're a fool."

Why was the hallucination insulting him? "Great, now the flying monkey's insulting me?"

He cleared his throat again. "A fool's mouth is his ruin, and his lips are a snare to himself."

Erik shook his head and let out a sigh. "Why can't you just answer a question?"

"Answer a fool according to his folly! Very well. You really should be thanking me," Vergis said. "You'll need to be alive if you want to get your brother back."

Erik's heart pounded in his chest. "Ozzie's alive?"

"He doesn't have much to offer the Stitcher. No, he's more interested in you," Vergis said, taking flight and landing on the hanging man's shoulder.

"Who's the Stitcher?"

"He's the one who made me."

Erik stood, but his vision blackened and his head felt empty. He tumbled to his hands and knees. "What does he want from me?"

"Same thing he took from me and all the others. He wants your parts."

Erik held a hand to his head and sat. He was still dizzy from the lack of oxygen. Maybe he was just delirious. But it all seemed too real to be a delusion. The eyes on Vergis' chest blinked. Delusion or not, it was still there talking to him. Its talons squeezed the dead man's shoulder. It looked dangerous. What made him different from the other Stitches? Why wasn't Vergis trying to kill him? Why could it talk?

"Can all the Stitches talk? You aren't like the others, are you?"

"Most of us lose that ability over time, but we all used to be human. Every animal part has a certain history to it, like a memory. My many eyes have seen so many things that it's really hard to tell what is my past and what isn't. My memories are like a giant stained glass window, only all the shards don't make one picture. They make many, but all the pieces are out of order. That's how it is for me anyway.

"Some Stitches have different parts and the animal instincts are more powerful than the human mind can handle. That's how it is for most of them. I still know I'm human, but most of them are no longer capable of thinking. Their soul, their mind, is trapped in a prison of stronger animal instincts."

Erik's stomach clamped. Every Stitch they'd seen used to be human? "Why is the human part of them weaker than the animal part, though?"

"Because of the pain," Vergis said. "It's really hard to think when you're suffering. The Stitcher cuts our bodies up and stitches different pieces together, pieces that should never go together, and it causes awful pain. The instinctual part of the body can handle that pain so much better than the mind. Pretty soon, the one replaces the other."

"Will he do that to Ozzie? Will he make him into a Stitch?"

"I don't know," Vergis said. "He might not, until he gets you."

"What does that matter?" Erik asked.

"He wants you. I know because it's my job to get you for him. But if he's got your brother, then he has something you want, something that will draw you to him."

Erik didn't like the idea of being butchered up like a pig, but the idea of being stitched up with parts of a pig was even worse. "What am I supposed to do? Everything I have done has turned out wrong. Everyone who followed me out here is dead. Knowing my luck, you're probably next."

Vergis nodded. "I probably am. That's why I never spoke to you before. I don't want the Stitcher to know I'm helping you." Vergis looked around the forest. "I'm not the only eyes in the skies he has and I will not help you anymore if I'm found out. It's just too dangerous."

The branches were still and there was only the quiet whisper of wind in the air. "I haven't seen anything. I think you're safe."

"I think so too, but we need to go."

"But how am I supposed to help my brother? I don't even have a weapon."

"Why do you think I brought you here? Look around. The dead man still has a couple knives and a sword. Take them and I'll show you where to go."

FORGOTTEN

Vergis' cave was cool in Erik's lungs. Vergis assured Erik that the cave was his own sanctuary and that no one knew about it. The wall was crudely painted with the most bizarre collage. Swashes of reds, blues, yellows, many pale and some vibrant were arranged like puzzle pieces.

"How long have you been painting this?" Erik asked.

"Three years now."

"Is this what your mind is like?"

"Not my mind, but my memory. That's why I can't remember details about my past, even my own name. No Stitch can."

Erik rounded his hand over the perimeter of the painting, a giant circle. There were swashes that looked like people and animals, but even those pictures were cut off into fragments. "What does it mean?" Erik asked.

"I don't know. My memories are strange. I don't see them in pictures; I feel them as emotions. Sometimes there are flashes of happiness or sadness, but it's hard to pin the feelings to events."

"Can I help?" Erik asked.

Vergis shook his head. "*I* can't even make sense of the painting. It's just a by-product of the Stitcher's work."

"The Stitcher..." Erik's hand fell from the painting. "Do you know where he is?"

"Of course. As a scout, I must report to him every few days."

"So you can take me to my brother?"

"No. I know where the Stitcher is, but I don't know where he keeps the Meat."

Meat? Warm blood coursed in his veins. What was he talking about? "My brother isn't meat."

"No, of course not. It's just what the Stitcher calls the animals and children he takes."

Erik shook his head. He'd thought Uncle Bauer was bad. Steinau and Uncle Bauer were a like dark hole, but Odenwald and the Stitcher were a bottomless pit. "Why doesn't he at least butcher bad people? Why does he have to take children?"

Vergis cleared his throat. "Folly is bound up in the heart of a child. They're easier to control than adults."

"What about you? He doesn't control you," Erik said.

Vergis sighed. "I'm no different. I've cooperated in his evil for years."

"But you're helping me."

Vergis cleared his throat. "He who says to the wicked, 'you are innocent,' will be cursed by peoples. No, I'm no hero. I have my own reasons for wanting to help you."

"As long as we get Ozzie back, you can have all the reasons you want. But how're we supposed to find him if you don't remember where the Stitcher holds...the Meat?"

Vergis looked at the painting on the wall and shook his head. "The answer's got to be in the mess on the wall. I was once just Meat myself. It's gotta be locked somewhere in my memory."

The painting was a maze of shards and half-images. Erik couldn't make sense of it. "I'm sorry, Vergis. I can't see anything."

Vergis cleared his throat. "The way of the wicked is like a deep darkness; they do not know over what they stumble."

"Why do you talk like that, Vergis? I don't understand."

A smile came to Vergis' face. He looked at Erik. "Those words are all cemented in my mind. I must have spent years memorizing them before I was a Stitch. They're not just a part of my memory, they're a part of me. They fight against the words of the Stitcher. They are how I know he's evil."

"But where do they come from?"

"I don't know, but they're sacred to me."

Erik stepped back. Even though the painting was disorganized, its colors and shapes were beautiful. None of it made sense, except the outline—the circle. "I think I see something," he said to Vergis.

Vergis spread out his wings and jumped closer to the painting. "Show me," he said. "What do you see?"

"No, no, no," Erik said. "Step back. Look at it from over here."

Vergis moved away from the wall, next to Erik. His eyes moved from shard to shard on the wall. Vergis shook his head. "I don't see it. What are you looking at?"

"All of it," Erik said. "Look, I don't know what all the little colors and pieces mean, but the whole shape, it's just like you said. It looks like a stained-glass window."

"I've always thought so, too. But what does that matter?" Vergis asked.

"Maybe your memories are linked up with a church, or monastery or something. Why else would your memory have that shape?"

Vergis nodded slowly and a smirk came to his face. He cleared his throat. "Does not wisdom call, does not understanding raise her voice?"

"Ozzie and I were heading for an old monastery when we set out. Maybe you stayed there before you were a Stitch? Maybe there're some clues there that could help you make sense of your memories."

"Maybe I was wrong to call you a fool after all," Vergis said. "That monastery isn't too far away, but it'll be dangerous. I should go alone."

Erik shook his head. "Not a chance. I can't just sit here and wait. Ozzie needs me."

"No. I can't risk being seen with you."

"I don't care. I have to save Ozzie. I'll be invisible, I promise."

Vergis scratched at the floor with his talons and cleared his throat. "The way of a fool is right in his own eyes, but a wise man listens to advice. If you follow me and get into trouble, I can't come to your aid."

"I understand. If I get attacked, I'll run."

Vergis shook his head. "There's no running away from them. You'll have to fight. Or die."

Erik shivered. Moonlight outlined the mountain's side. Like the hairs on an old man's head, the trees were less numerous and grew farther apart. The stars shimmered in the black sky better than Erik'd ever seen. The terrain, however, was rocky and difficult. He scaled over a small cliff, always keeping an eye on Vergis. He was careful to follow from a distance, though. Vergis was his only chance to find Ozzie.

The wind chilled Erik's lungs and it smelled like rain. It still hurt to breath, but Ozzie's being alive compensated for it. Maybe it was still all his fault, but at least now he could make some of it right. He just needed to find him and get him out of Odenwald.

Vergis perched on a distant branch. They weren't there yet, which meant Vergis was waiting for Erik to climb another obstacle. The cliff had a difficult incline and there weren't many rocks or roots to grab and hoist himself up on. It didn't help that it was almost pitch black. He was lucky to at least have the full moon. He walked alongside the wall and felt for a good anchor. He found a rock and lifted himself up, but it crumbled under his weight. He crashed to the ground and let out a grunt. His chest still hurt from his first attack from the Stitch that took his brother.

He scrambled to his feet and resumed his search.

A rustling from the nearby bush startled him. He turned around. Light reflected off two tiny eyes in the dark. He drew his sword and steadied it in front of him. The creature growled. The outline of a fox emerged in the moonlight. No, it was a wolf. The two glimmering lights multiplied as the moonlight was reflected by the teeth of the creature.

"Stay back," Erik said. He slashed the air in front of him.

The creature barked back.

Erik stumbled back against the wall. Vergis was right—there'd be no running away this time, and Jonas wasn't there to save him either. He gripped the hilt of the sword, took a deep breath and ran forward. The creature leapt out of the way. Erik swung and missed, stumbled forward, and tripped to his knees. The creature pounced into his back. Erik swiveled and swung the sword in an arc behind him. The blade sliced into rough flesh.

The monster fell back and groaned. Erik jumped to his feet and turned. The creature cowered on the ground. Its legs shook like an old man's hands. Something strange was on its back. It looked like another leg, but it was too dark. Erik edged closer, sword in front of him. It coiled back.

Erik crept closer.

The Stitch lunged at him. Erik swung, but the creature was too fast. It clawed at his stomach, and Erik toppled to the ground, dropping his sword. He grabbed at the Stitch to throw it off, but the additional limb on its back made it difficult to grab. It wasn't hairy like the Stitch's body; it was limp and heavy.

A shriek came from over Erik. Vergis descended and grabbed the Stitch with its talons. He pulled it to the ground. Erik took a knife from his belt and plunged it into the Stitch's neck. He jerked it violently until the Stitch lay still.

Erik removed the blade and wiped it in the grass. He wheezed for a minute and struggled to his feet. "Thanks Vergis," he whispered.

Vergis flew off without a word.

The weird limb stuck out from the Stitch's furry body. What was on its back that was so smooth? He crouched and lifted it up into the moonlight.

Erik gasped.

It wasn't a leg at all; it was an arm. It was cold and grey, and there was a message stitched into it: "HIM FOR YOU." Erik dropped the arm and bent over. Was it Ozzie's arm?. He shot his hand into his pocket and squeezed. Cold tears trickled down his face.

He inhaled and blew out the blood-tainted air. He released his rock.

"HIM FOR YOU."

What did that mean? Maybe Vergis would know more. At the very least, maybe it meant Ozzie was still alive, and if so, Erik was going to find him.

He scaled the rock wall. Vergis flew ahead. A fluttering of wings whispered behind Erik. A weight released in his stomach. Were they being tracked?

Vergis really wasn't the only eyes in the skies.

STAINED GLASS

The monastery nestled into the rock cliff, but jutted out from the wall like a jagged tooth. Vergis glided through a broken window. Erik shoved open the heavy wooden door.

While the door was huge, the monastery was smaller than he'd imagined. It was little more than a tiny chapel with five small rooms along the side. He entered the nearest room. There were two holes hewn out of the rock face. They were sleeping quarters. The "beds" were like small coffins. Erik'd never felt it before, but he now understood the meaning of claustrophobia. Uncle Bauer's barn was like a mansion compared to the monks' quarters.

He exited and found Vergis standing on the altar.

"You killed that Stitch back there, right?" Vergis asked.

Earlier it wouldn't have bothered Erik, but now that he knew Stitches used to be human, it did. "I had to. It was going to kill me."

Vergis nodded. "Good, that way it can't report back to the Stitcher. But still, it's a pity."

Erik didn't know how it would've communicated with the Stitcher, but *it* wasn't the one he was afraid would report back. It was the bird that flew away after he'd killed the Stitch that worried him. But he couldn't tell Vergis; he needed his help. Besides, it could've just been a regular bird. "Your secret is safe. That monster won't be reporting to anyone now."

Erik's fingers singed with heat. Lying didn't come easy, especially since Vergis was glaring at him. Could he tell?

Vergis' head cocked to the side.

Erik's heart pounded. "What are you staring at?"

"Turn around and see for yourself."

He did. Moonlight illuminated a rounded stained-glass window. Its colors were dim, but the contrasts in the shards converged in the middle with a white lamb holding a flag in its leg. It stood on an altar and a pale red stream of blood gushed from its side onto it. Its eyes were focused, and its expression was serious. "What is it?" Erik asked.

"Look at the shape," Vergis said.

The rounded window and segmented pieces were familiar. "It's like your picture."

"It is, except that, unlike mine, it's not all out of order."

Out of order or not, it didn't make any sense to Erik. Nothing did, least of all the message stitched into his brother's severed arm. "Vergis, I saw something earlier when I killed that Stitch. There was a message that said, 'him for you.' Does that mean anything to you?"

Vergis shook his head. "Sounds like terms of a bargain. It sounds like he wants you."

If it meant Ozzie could be saved, Erik would do it. "Maybe I should accept the de—"

"No. Don't *ever* trust him," Vergis said.

Erik sighed and ground his teeth. Vergis' eyes never left the window. What did he see in it? "I'm still confused. What does the window tell you?"

"I can't remember, but I do know this place. It's like déjà vu. I must have been here before." He hopped around the altar, looking around the chapel. "I wonder if I left anything here."

"Maybe you stayed in one of those little rooms," Erik said. "I'll check them out."

"Good, I'll look around here," Vergis said.

Erik scoured the rooms. He ran his hands in the small niches in the walls, but found nothing. In the final room he discovered a ripped newspaper article tucked away.

Vergis searched the rocky ground underneath the altar. Erik held out the newspaper. "Is this useful?"

"What does it say?" Vergis asked.

To Erik, it was just columns of mostly meaningless marks. There were very few words he recognized. "I don't know what it says," he said. "I can't read so well."

"But didn't you say you saw a message earlier?"

Erik nodded. "There was this girl, Lara, that taught me a little, but I only know some words. When my cousin found out she was teaching me, he told Uncle Bauer. He said if I had time to read, I wasn't doing enough work." Warmth swelled in Erik's face. "After that I never got to spend time with Lara. All I wanted to do was read Ozzie the stories from Mom's book…"

Vergis nodded. "Hold the article out for me. I'll read it."

Erik held it in front of Vergis.

"A girl from Wiesthal was burned at the stake for the crime of witchcraft. This practice, all but abolished in enlightened societies, still exists in small communities steeped in superstitious belief. Rosaline was blamed for a plague that devastated the town. She was forced from her home, beaten, tied and burned at the stake. Predictably, her remaining family members moved from Wiesthal and were unavailable for comment."

"I don't get it," Erik said.

Vergis shook his head. "Me either. It's probably just trash. But I think I know where to look. I was drawn to this altar for a while and I couldn't explain why. If you look at the picture on the window there are bones under the altar. I seem to remember that relics are sometimes buried under altars. I can't be sure, but I feel like I may have buried something here. Can you move some of these stones for me?"

Erik dropped the article and lifted a few rocks. Hidden beneath them was a small black book. Erik dug it out and thumbed through the pages. Many were blank, but there were hand-written notes on a number of pages. "Does this look familiar?"

Vergis' attention shot to the door. He whispered, "Do you hear that?"

Erik froze. There was faint tapping from outside the monastery.

"Footsteps," Vergis whispered. "Hide." He grabbed the book in his talons and flew inside one of the small rooms.

The steps drew closer. Erik squatted behind the altar and unsheathed his sword.

The door creaked open.

Erik held his breath and peered to the side of the altar. A figure ducked behind the pews. Erik tightened his hand around the hilt and hid himself.

Something dashed swiftly on the hard floor, approaching the altar.

Erik gasped. It must've seen him.

"Don't move," a voice said.

Erik darted around the altar.

Nils shouted, "Stop there!" His rifle was aimed at Erik.

Erik dropped his sword and held up his hands. "Whoa! Nils, it's me, Erik. Put the gun down."

Nils squinted and lowered the rifle. "Erik? What're you doing here?"

"I...uh..."

"Is Jonas here too? I thought I heard voices." Nils looked around the monastery.

Erik swallowed. He shook his head. "Jonas was killed. I'm...I'm alone."

"I'm sorry. Why are you here?" Nils asked, searching the monastery.

"I'm trying to find my brother. What about you?"

"I set up here for the last few hours. This place seems pretty safe." Nils approached the sleeping quarters.

Erik couldn't let him find Vergis. There was no way he'd understand. Erik'd have to be quick to knock him out. He knelt down and retrieved his sword. The newspaper article was on the floor also, which gave him a less dangerous idea. "Hey, is this yours?"

Nils' attention moved to Erik. He walked to him and took the article. "Yeah, it's mine. Did you read it?"

"Um...yeah, I read it. But, I don't really know what it's all about."

Nils lounged on the wooden pews. Erik mimicked him. "Before my dad and I came here, we went around to as many towns as we could looking for stories about the Stitcher. We found that the town with the earliest and most abductions was Wiesthal. The locals insisted it all started with the burning of a girl named Rosaline."

Erik shook his head. "I still don't understand."

"They believe that Rosaline's father started abducting their children for revenge. They killed his daughter, so he took their children. He probably killed them and buried them in the forest."

It was an interesting theory, but it didn't make sense. "Ozzie and I live in Steinau. We don't even have relatives in Wiesthal. But he took Ozzie and I'm pretty sure he wants me too."

Nils looked down and back at Erik, nodding. "And the girl I'm looking for is from Erbach. I don't know why he goes after others now. Maybe it's become like an addiction for him."

Erik stood up. "Do you know where he keeps them?"

Nils stretched out on the pew and sighed. "Not yet, but I know it's close."

Quiet tapping came from one of the rooms and Vergis' head peaked out. How could Erik get him out without Nils noticing?

Nils shot up. He whispered, "Did you hear that?"

Could he tell him the truth? That he'd befriended a Stitch? No, if Vergis wanted Nils to know, he wouldn't be hiding right now. "It's noth—"

SWOOSH!

Vergis jetted through the air and perched on the ledge of the stained-glass window. He grasped the small book in his talons and looked at Nils.

"Look out!" Nils yelled, jumping to his feet. He grabbed his rifle and targeted Vergis. "Don't move, Stitch!"

Vergis slipped out through a hole in the glass.

"Damn," Nils muttered. "Follow me. We gotta kill it before it compromises our location." Nils sprinted out the door.

Erik followed Nils out of the monastery. The trees were empty. He didn't hear any fluttering.

"Did you see it?" Nils asked.

He didn't, but he had an idea where Vergis'd be going.

"Yeah," Erik said. "He went east. He's along the rocks." It was a lie, but he'd have to send Nils the wrong direction. That way Vergis would be free to travel west to his cave.

Nils ran, but Erik held back.

"What're you waiting for? We don't have time to waste here," Nils said.

"Just go, I've got my own mission."

Nils fired down the path eastward. "Your funeral."

Twenty minutes wasted and no sign of the bird. Nils slowed his jog and slung his rifle over his shoulder. The trees thinned and the sky glowed in morning red and orange. The sun idled over a hill a few kilometers away. He leaned on a wooden fence that stretched from Nils all the way to the top of the hill, where an old farmhouse stood silhouetted in the red sky.

Could that be the place? His father said the Stitcher was near and Nils had investigated the area plenty. The building rose from the ground a few meters and had stairs up to the porch. The walls were brown and aged like a rotting tree. The windows were haphazardly boarded over from the inside. His flesh went cold and goose bumps prickled over his arms. Was Pia there? He breathed to calm himself. It might be abandoned. But then again, there was no telling what he might find inside.

He didn't want to go alone. He wished his father were alive and with him, or even Erik. But he'd gone the other way. Why had Erik done that? It didn't make sense. After all, Nils had a rifle. All Erik had was a sword. Why would he want to split up? Probably just to get away from the Stitch, but, if he's looking for his brother, following the Stitch is what he'd want to do.

He inhaled the chilled air, and prowled forward. He idly traced the wood of the fence, his gaze cemented on the building. His foot snagged on a rock. His fingers slipped from the fence and he toppled to the ground.

He groaned and kicked the obstacle. It groaned back at him.

Nils scampered away and aimed his rifle at the mound. Its shape moved in the shadows. "Get back," Nils said.

Its contours came into view. Legs, torso, arm...it was a boy. The youth held his head, groaned, and stood up. He had a bloody stump where one arm should've been. Fear gripped the boy's eyes when they settled on Nils' rifle. He put his hand forward. "W-wait. Don't shoot."

He wasn't a Stitch and didn't appear dangerous, so Nils lowered his rifle. "Who are you?"

The boy covered his stomach. "I'm Ozzie. Who're you?"

"Wait. Did you say Ozzie? Weren't you captured by the Stitcher? How'd you get away? Did you see a girl there?"

Ozzie scratched his head and rubbed his face.

"Sorry," Nils said. "Let's slow down. I'm Nils. What happened to you?"

Ozzie exhaled a long breath. "Um...yeah, I was taken by the Stitcher. He cut off my arm and...um..." Ozzie's eyes surveyed the landscape. "Have you seen my brother, Erik? Or Jonas?"

"Please," Nils said, "before I answer that, you gotta tell me, was there a girl there too?"

Ozzie furrowed his brow and nodded, like he was beginning to remember. "Yes. It was just me and this girl and a lot of dead animal parts everywhere. He cut her eyes out and she was blindfolded."

"Was her name Pia?"

"She was too afraid to talk. She said something about being called Meat, but I don't think that's her real name. Now can you tell me about Erik and Jonas?"

Nils nodded. "I promise I will, but first you gotta tell me how you got out of there? Did the girl get out too?"

Ozzie stared at the ground. "I don't know. The last thing I remember was being taken out of my cage and the Stitcher took me to his table where he cuts up the animals."

"What about the girl?"

He shook his head. "I'm sorry. I don't remember."

"Okay. Thanks for the information," Nils said, withdrawing a knife from his belt.

Ozzie jumped back. "Hey, wait!" he screamed. "What're you doing?"

"No, no, no," Nils said. "Take it easy. I'm not gonna kill you. Take the knife, it's dangerous out there."

Ozzie blew out his breath. "You scared me. I was really beginning to lose my faith in strangers."

"Your instincts are good. Out here, you can't trust anyone," Nils said, putting the knife in Ozzie's hand.

"What about my brother and Jonas? Have you seen them?"

"I just saw your brother about half an hour ago. He's west of here."

Ozzie's eyes brightened and he smiled. "And Jonas is with him?"

Nils shook his head. "You'll have to ask your brother about it, but I think he's dead."

Ozzie's smile disappeared. He took a couple steps away, but turned back. "Will you help me find my brother?"

It would be the right thing to do, but Nils needed to get Pia before it was too late. Besides, the Stitcher might be tracking Ozzie, and he didn't want to be around when things got bad. "Sorry, I can't help you. I have to do what I came here to do. Keep your eyes open though."

Ozzie sighed. "Okay. Thanks for the knife."

MEAT

The Stitcher had taken his twin sister, and Hannes would kill him for it. He slipped out of the rectory at night. Father Neumann wouldn't approve of his plan. Killing was forbidden by the Law of Moses, and Hannes agreed. But Moses was talking about killing humans. The Stitcher was a demon.

Problem was, they'd never ordain Hannes if he killed the Stitcher, but maybe Emelia would be alive and the curse that darkened Odenwald would be gone. That would be a good enough exchange. The rain erupted from drops to showers. The pounding of the water would help to conceal his footsteps. He didn't know what penalty there'd be for getting caught, but Fr Neumann wouldn't go easy on him.

He pulled his cloak over his head and cassock and trudged past the first few trees of Odenwald armed with a lantern and a knife. The forest was black and noisy with crickets and owls. He plodded carefully into the dark.

A voice shattered the night from behind. "Hannes! Stop."

How'd they know? It didn't matter, there was no sense going back now. Hannes burst into a sprint.

BANG!

The gunshot startled Hannes, and he collapsed to the ground.

"Don't take another step," came a familiar voice—Fr Neumann.

Hannes pushed himself up and turned. Fr Neumann stood at the edge of the forest. His chest was bare and pale, as were his legs. He wore only a pair of shorts. He shivered as a wisp of cloud escaped his mouth, rain dripping from his bald head. He held a rifle in his hands. He was no fool.

"How'd you know I'd be here?" Hannes asked.

"I'm not half as stupid as you think. Monsignor knew you'd come out here the second that Petersen boy showed up."

"It's a sign from God, Father. He's the only one I've ever heard escaped the Stitcher, and he found *us*. I can't let this chance go to waste. Please, let me go."

"Monsignor gave strict orders to all of us to watch you. If I let you go, it'll all be on me."

"I'm sorry about that," Hannes said. "But you're not really going to shoot me if I go, are you?"

"Do you really want to find out?"

"I don't really have a choice, do I?"

"Hannes, you're no fool. You know the stakes involved here. You'll never get ordained if you leave."

"Yes Father, I know. But I have to try."

"Last chance," Fr Neumann said, rifle aimed at Hannes.

"You'll have to shoot. It's the only way to stop me."

Fr Neumann sighed. "Very well." He lowered the rifle and tossed it to Hannes. "Godspeed."

Hannes cleared his throat. "The Lord's curse is on the house of the wicked, but he blesses the home of the righteous."

He knew exactly where to go—a seemingly abandoned farmhouse not too far from an old Benedictine monastery. The Petersen boy wrote it down for him in his book. He hastened as the rain pounded on him. After an hour he reached the monastery. It would be his shelter for the night.

He slipped in and sat at a pew. He opened his book and checked the directions. He would set out after getting some sleep. He would need his energy.

He admired the stained-glass window as he prayed for strength. The lamb in the middle of the window held a flag of victory, but also bled from his side. For the lamb, success and defeat were entwined.

But not for Hannes.

Should he fail it would be good to leave a witness of his mission. He wrote down his plans in the book and placed it under the stones of the altar, where the remains of martyrs were often kept.

Erik stretched and cracked his back. Pain shot like lightning up his body. The rock floor of Vergis' cave made him long for home. A pile of hay, a blanket, and a room with a bunch of pigs looked pretty good to him now, as long as Ozzie was there with him.

Vergis was awake. He stood on top of the small black book and turned its pages beneath his talons.

"So can you read ten times faster with that many eyes?" Erik asked.

Vergis shook his head and cleared his throat. "Answer not a fool according to his folly, lest you be like him yourself."

Vergis' words of wisdom were not a first-thing-in-the-morning kind of thing. "Okay, fine," Erik said. "Stupid question. But really, why did the Stitcher give you so many eyes?"

"For tracking. Some of them are eagle's eyes; they let me see great distances. I also have wolf and owl eyes that allow me to see better in the dark.

"That sounds useful," Erik said.

"It may sound like a good thing, but all his gifts come at a price. I have to go to him tonight and give the report. And get fixed."

He had to return to the Stitcher...to get fixed? Erik still hadn't told Vergis about them being seen last night. "You can't go," Erik said.

"I have to."

"Can't you just hide here? You said yourself that no one knows about this place."

Vergis closed the book and looked at Erik. "It's not that easy. The Stitcher's work is never done. He poisons parts of each of us. I'm always in need of repair. If I don't go back and get fixed, I will die."

"So that's how he controls you?"

"Me and all the others. He builds weaknesses into each Stitch and he knows how to exploit them. Sometimes it's overt like a horn through a leg. Sometimes it's interior and hidden, like mine. But he knows how to exploit them, so no one can revolt. Most of us end up fighting for approval so that he will ease our pain."

"But not you?"

Vergis shook his head and looked down.

"And you're going back tonight?"

"Either that or die."

Erik seized the rock in this pocket. If the bird he'd heard was a scout, Vergis was gonna die no matter what. He couldn't hide it any longer; Vergis deserved to know. "I...I uh...I heard something the other night...after I killed the Stitch." Erik sighed. "I think something saw you help me."

Vergis scratched his talons against the rock floor. He nodded slowly and cleared his throat. "Faithful are the wounds of a friend; profuse are the kisses of an enemy."

Erik had expected to be yelled at. Maybe he'd spent too much of his life with Uncle Bauer, but he still didn't feel like Vergis should be so gracious. "How can you call me a friend? I lied to you. It's not right."

Vergis cleared his throat "He who—"

Erik shouted, "Stop it! Don't quote some book. Tell me how you really feel."

Vergis flung out his wings with a swoosh. Erik jumped back against the wall. "These words are the only reason I help you. Since I have lost my memories, they are my only way of knowing myself besides what the Stitcher tells me. Don't tell me not to say them. They are all that is left of my identity."

Erik's heart raced. His hands hurt from grasping the stony wall. "On second thought, you just recite all the lines you like," Erik said.

Vergis lowered his wings and returned to the book.

"Are you still going to help me find Ozzie?"

Vergis nodded. "I told you I wouldn't help if the Stitcher found out, but I've changed my mind."

"Why?"

"Because of this book. It was my journal."

A light rustling echoed in the cave from outside.

"What? Really? What does it say?" Erik asked.

"Shhh." Vergis glided to the entrance.

Erik inched toward him and whispered, "What is it?" Outside were bushes on the horizon and branches above. But it all looked peaceful to him.

Vergis soared out and alighted on a tree branch. Was it Nils? The last thing Erik needed was for Nils to come back. Then again, a Stitch would be worse. He grabbed his sword.

Vergis shouted, "Erik, come here!"

Erik was shocked that Vergis would be so loud, but then he saw why. Ozzie was wandering through the foliage! He stumbled about like he was drunk, but that didn't matter. He was alive. He was free.

"Ozzie, come here. Hurry." Erik sprinted out to meet him and embraced him. Ozzie's arm was gone, replaced with a bloody stump. Erik supported him into the cave.

Ozzie's hand grasped a knife; he held it against his stomach. His face was pale, but his smile was wide. So was Erik's. Now they'd be able to leave this godforsaken forest.

Vergis flew in and landed a couple meters away. Ozzie's eyes went wild. "Erik, look out!" He held his knife out and dashed forward.

"Whoa! Ozzie, it's okay," Erik said, pushing him back and standing between him and Vergis. "This is Vergis. He's a good guy."

"But it's a monster!" Ozzie said.

Vergis hopped forward. "I'm not like the others. I'm not going to hurt you." Vergis' head cocked to the side. "What happened to your arm?"

Ozzie collapsed back as if he'd been shot. "N-n-n...did it just talk?"

"It's okay, Ozzie," Erik said.

Ozzie's mouth hung open, but no words came out. His eyes darted between Vergis and Erik.

"Just breathe," Erik said. "Now, did the Stitcher do that to you?"

Ozzie nodded.

"Why?" Erik asked.

"He said my arm was infected, so he cut it off before it killed me."

"Why would he want to save you?" Erik asked.

"I don't know, but we gotta go ba—"

"He saved him to lure you to him," Vergis said to Erik. "Remember the message? Him for you."

Erik nodded. "But now he's safe. We can just leave."

"No. We have to go back," Ozzie said.

"What are you talking about? We should get out of here," Erik said.

Vergis stepped closer. "You can't leave now. We have to kill the Stitcher."

"And save the girl," Ozzie said.

"What girl?" Erik asked.

"There was a girl there too. We can't just leave her."

"Can't she save herself," Erik asked. "I mean, you did, right?"

Ozzie's face hardened. "I don't…I don't know."

"What? How do you not know?" Erik asked.

Ozzie shook his head.

"It doesn't matter," Vergis said. "Unless you kill the Stitcher, he's gonna hunt you down. Running away's only a temporary solution."

"But Vergis, if we kill the Stitcher, won't that mean you'll die too?"

Vergis nodded. "I'm as good as dead anyway. That's why I told you I'd help you save Ozzie even if the Stitcher knows I'm helping you. Three years ago I left everything to kill him. Now that I know who I am, I'm not afraid to die."

"The bird's right," Ozzie said. "We gotta go back to save the girl, too. That's what Mom would do."

Erik shook his head. Mom ended up dying before her time. Erik didn't want that fate for Ozzie. But he did owe Vergis. He'd protected Erik from the beginning. But now that Ozzie was here everything was different. They'd be safe in a big place like Lohr. They could start life over and be happy again. Vergis wouldn't like it, but he'd have to respect it. "No. We're not going back. Ozzie and I are going to Lohr, just like we planned."

Vergis flashed his wings. "You can't just—"

"*We* didn't plan it," Ozzie interrupted. "*You* planned it and made me come out here even though I never wanted to. Now look at me!" He motioned to his stump.

Erik's face heated and sweat percolated on his skin. Ozzie was right. He reached for his rock.

Ozzie continued, "Do what you want, but I'm going back with the bird. I'll kill the Stitcher myself if I have to!"

Ozzie was insane. Erik'd just got him back and he already wanted to put himself back in danger. How did he plan to kill the Stitcher as pale and weak as he was, and with one arm?

"Erik," Vergis spoke, "this isn't going to stop until he's dead. No matter where you go, he's not going to leave you alone. We have to end it."

"Is this the place?" Erik asked.

"Yeah, this is where I woke up," Ozzie said.

It didn't rub Erik the right way that Ozzie just woke up here. They'd decided that the Stitcher thought he was dead and just dumped him, but Erik had his doubts.

They crawled behind the brush. A farmhouse loomed about fifty meters away. The stench of rotting meat tainted the air, and turned Erik's stomach to jelly. How long had Ozzie suffered there? He didn't want to think about it.

Near the steps leading to the porch, Erik spotted a Stitch about the size of a wolf. It sat with its warthog head resting on its paws. Unfortunately, Vergis wouldn't be able to help him this time; he'd already gone to report to the Stitcher.

The Stitch's head shot up and it sniffed the air.

Erik whispered, "Lay low a sec." He lay flat behind the brush.

Ozzie obeyed.

The Stitch rested its head as if satisfied that nothing was unusual. The smell from the house must've been too overpowering.

"How d'we get past it?" Ozzie asked.

"I'm not sure," Erik said, gripping his sword. "But we may have to fight."

"I don't know if I can help much," Ozzie said.

"What're you talking about? You still have one good arm, don't ya?"

Ozzie chuckled quietly, but then coughed.

"Shh—"

The Stitch jumped up. Erik pulled Ozzie to the ground and hit his own head on a stone. It hurt like a stubbed toe, but he bit his tongue.

After a minute of silence, they sat up, still hidden in the brush. The Stitch was pacing the perimeter of the house, sniffing the ground.

Erik whispered, "No more mistakes like that, Ozzie."

Ozzie nodded.

Erik rubbed his head and picked up the rock. "I have a plan." He smiled at Ozzie. "Let's have it chase a ghost in the forest."

Ozzie smirked. "You sure you can throw it far enough?"

"Not a problem," Erik whispered. "I've got a great arm, no offense." The Stitch turned its back, nose to the ground. Erik stood. He'd only have one chance. He gripped the rock and hurled it as far as he could into the trees behind the farmhouse. The Stitch's head shot up at the sound and it crashed off after the echoes.

Ozzie whispered, "Wow! Nice throw!"

"In and out as fast as possible."

He and Ozzie sprinted up the stairs to the door. Erik thrust it open. The smell hit him like a fist, but he crept into the darkness.

THREADING

Nils fought to sunder the ropes that tied his hands, but they were too tight and sturdy. Again he was immobilized, this time tied to a pillar inside a barn. He hadn't even made it into the farmhouse before he was ambushed. It wasn't that he wasn't ready. He saw the Stitch from across the field. He had his gun trained on it as he crept close for the kill shot.

No, it was the Stitch that trailed behind him that got him. He never fired a shot or swung a knife, and now he was weaponless again. But now it wasn't just some crazy man looking for his son in the woods. Now he was caught by the Stitcher himself.

He wasn't at all like Nils expected. He thought of him like a shadowy monster or maybe a huge gorilla-shaped man with a blood-stained butcher's apron. The tall, thin man in front of him looked more like a professor or a librarian. Thick glasses, black pants, tan shirt. He was just a normal guy. A normal *looking* guy, anyway.

The man lifted Nils' head with a firm finger under his chin. He squinted as he looked into Nils' eyes, and shook his head. "Useless," he said. "Just another useless piece of meat."

Useless? Before him was the man responsible for his father's death, and he just added insult to injury. Nils spat in his face.

"If anything's useless, it's you."

The man took a rag from his pocket and wiped his cheek. He returned the rag and withdrew a knife. He held the tiny blade to Nils' neck, suspending it just over his skin.

"Over the years, I've developed a skill," the man started. "I can find your greatest weakness and cut into it minute after minute, day after day, and never let it stop." He pushed the blade into Nils' shoulder. Nils shouted and jolted back and forth, but couldn't escape.

He withdrew the knife and seized Nils' shoulders to force him still.

"You know how dogs learn?" the Stitcher asked. He glided the knife down to Nil's hand. "You must train them with pain." He pushed the knife into Nils' pinky.

Tears burst from Nils' eyes and a shriek exploded out of him. He flailed, but his bonds held him securely. The rope burned against his wrists, but like everything else, they were immobile.

The Stitcher removed the blade and put it away. He retrieved the rag from his pocket, bunched it up and shoved it into Nils' mouth. "Of course with humans these things shouldn't be necessary," the Stitcher said. "We'll see whether you're smarter than a dog."

Nils' hand throbbed as the blood trickled down and dripped on his leg. The rag was moist and tasted like dust. He wanted to rain down razor-blade spit on the Stitcher and burn his body. He'd be happy to shoot him or cut him, or anything else. But there was nothing he could do.

An owl-like Stitch alighted on the sill of an old window and entered through a broken pane. It was a hideous sight. An owl full of eyes with a monkey's face. Its head cocked to the side when it saw him.

The Stitcher held up his hand as if warning the Stitch to come no closer. It swooped to the floor and lowered its head to him. "I've been waiting for you," the Stitcher said.

Nils couldn't believe what happened next. He was sure the bird spoke back.

"Here I am. What do you wish to know?"

The Stitcher stepped toward the bird and withdrew his small knife. He pointed it at Nils. "Is this the Meat you've found for me?"

The bird looked Nils in the eyes. "No, he's not the one."

The Stitcher towered over the creature. "Then where is the one I need? There's been rumors that you've spoken to him." He knelt down, grabbed the bird by the neck, and held the knife to its throat. "Is it true?"

The Stitch stiffened. "I've convinced him to follow me to you."

"That's not your decision to make. You're just the scout. The others bring him to me, not you."

"You mean like last time? They brought you the wrong one! I'm at least smart enough to bring the one you want."

"Then where is he?"

"He's gone to rescue the girl in the cage."

He threw the Stitch back, shot up and rubbed his chin. "He's there right now?"

The creature jumped to its talons. "Yes sir, and I'm sure you have the place secure?"

The Stitcher looked at Nils, then turned away. His gaze made Nils' stomach jump inside him. "Of the two guards, only one is there. The other is here. He brought me this worthless Meat." He turned to the bird. "Go there and make sure they're delayed. I'll be on my way personally."

"Yes sir," the bird said and spread its wings. It jumped but landed again and looked at the Stitcher.

"What are you waiting for?" he asked.

"You haven't cut it out yet."

The Stitcher smirked, then knelt down and dug his knife into its neck, hollowing out one of its eyes.

The bird whimpered. Nils hung his head. It was too much to watch. The Stitch fluttered away.

"Follow him," the Stitcher said. "From a distance. Don't let anyone see you."

An eagle dropped from the rafters and flew out the window as well.

The Stitcher turned to Nils and walked toward him, pocketing the dismembered eye. "You're coming with me."

Erik swallowed. He had to hold down the vomit. At first he thought it was the smell, but it wasn't. It was the gnats swirling around the long-forgotten animal limbs. It was the table with its assortment of knives—big, small, serrated or smooth, but all stained brown and black. And it was the cages. Two were empty, but one had a pitiful looking girl in it. Erik crept to her cage, Ozzie behind him. He grabbed the cage-door, but it was locked tight.

"Alright Ozzie, let's get her out. Do you have the key?"

The girl slapped his hands. "What're you doing? Get away."

Erik rubbed his hands. "It's okay. We're here to rescue you. Ozzie, the key?"

"The Stitcher has it," Ozzie said.

Erik turned to his brother. "Are you kidding? Why'd we come here if you don't have it? We can't just wait here. That Stitch will only be chasing the rock for so long."

Ozzie shook his head. "Don't be an idiot. There's a saw over on the Stitcher's table. We can cut the bars."

The table was full of knives, but the hacksaw would be all he needed. He felt stupid, and Ozzie's half-smile didn't help. He nodded and dashed to the table. He grabbed the saw and returned to the cage.

"Scoot back," Erik said to the girl. "I'm gonna cut the cage open."

She coiled back and Erik sawed the metal bars. They weren't too thick, but it wouldn't be like slicing through butter either. "Ozzie, keep an eye on the door. This is going to take a minute."

Within a few seconds the saw cut through the top of two bars. "Hang in there. We'll have you out in no time," Erik said, moving the saw lower.

"Aren't you afraid the Stitcher'll find you?" she asked.

"He's busy with a friend of mine right now. We'll be out of here long before he shows up."

"You'd better be right," she said.

The bars gave way and clanked on the ground. "We don't have time to cut any more bars. Take my hand. You should be able to fit through."

"Erik," Ozzie said, closing the door. "We have a problem." He dashed back and held his knife in front of him. "Something's coming."

Erik grabbed the girl's hand. "Hurry!" He pulled her from the cage and moved her behind him, still brandishing the saw.

The door shook with a thud. A voice came from the other side. "Erik, it's Vergis. Open the door. Quickly!"

"Ozzie, open the door," Erik said.

Ozzie put his knife away and pulled the door open. Vergis flew in. His neck was stained red. "He's coming. You gotta get out of here."

"Shit," Erik said. "Okay, we're done here anyway. Let's go." He dropped the Stitcher's saw, grabbed the girl's hand and led her out the door. The stairs leading down from the porch wouldn't be easy for her. He lifted her up and carried her down the steps. Vergis glided down to meet him.

The warthog-Stitch grunted from behind the house. His fool's errand must've come to an end. They'd be able to run, but there was no time for mistakes.

"Where's Ozzie?" Vergis asked.

The girl stood next to him, but Ozzie wasn't there. The stairs were empty too. Was he still in there? "I thought he was right behind me."

Ozzie sprinted out the door.

"What're you doing?" Erik yelled. "C'mon!"

The Stitch rounded the right side of the house. Its grunting turned to growling when it saw them.

Ozzie bounded down the steps. Erik snatched the knife out of Ozzie's hand and slapped the girl's hand into his. "Get her out of here." He slid the knife in Ozzie's belt. "Vergis, take them to the cave. I'll meet up with you when I'm done here."

Ozzie protested, but Erik shoved him. "Go!"

Vergis soared away. Ozzie shouted, "Versteck," and fled off with the girl.

Versteck? The pan-hiding game? What was Ozzie talking about?

The Warthog Stitch raced at Erik. Its eyes burned pain. It sped at him like a bullet. Erik braced himself. The creature pounced at him, but Erik collapsed flat to the ground. The Stitch tumbled over him, tripping face-first into the rocky path. Erik shot up and lunged, stabbing its hind leg. It screamed and scrambled to its paws, its wounded wolf-leg bent and dangling.

At least he'd crippled it. It'd allow more time for Ozzie to distance himself from the beast. The Stitch turned and aimed its tusks at him.

It rushed forward, limping only slightly. It must've been running on pure adrenaline, but Erik would make it suffer. He bolted for the steps leaping two and three at a time. The sound of claws scraping into wood filled the air behind him. He ran inside and grabbed a handful of knives. He returned to find the beast struggling half-way up the stairs, growling.

He lifted a knife up to his eye, zeroed in on the Stitch and launched it. It slashed into the creature's shoulder. It shrieked and tumbled down a step.

He threw a second, but missed.

He wouldn't miss again. He raised the third knife and flung it at its head. The blade cut into its eye. The Stitch wailed and thrashed the wood of the steps with its claws. It climbed all the faster now that it was wild with pain.

Erik retreated into the dark room, slammed the door and crouched behind a pile of limbs. The smell was awful, but at least it would keep the Stitch off his scent. And since he'd nearly blinded it, it'd have to find him like a needle in a haystack.

The beast crashed into the door. It was secure, but it couldn't hold for long. Cages and piles of animal parts were everywhere, but he found nothing useful. He took out his blade and waited.

The second thud came with a crack of wood splintering. The third crash demolished the door. Shards of wood flew past him. The creature tromped through the room swiping piles and trampling over animal carcasses. Heat coursed through Erik's fingers. The Stitch wouldn't find him like a needle in a haystack. It was going to burn down the haystack and get the needle by happenstance.

A severed leg of a deer tumbled next to Erik. He swiped it and lobbed it into the corner of the room, next to the Stitcher's worktable. It thudded against the wall. The monster charged after the sound. He couldn't believe it worked a second time. He darted the other way.

He sprinted for the opening in the door, but there was something behind it. There was only one thing to do: Erik lowered his shoulders and burst through the opening. The obstacle was a man, and behind him was Nils, bound in rope. The man caught Erik by the throat and flung him down to the floorboards. His head crashed against the wood, shattering his vision into shimmering dots on a black landscape. His hand felt empty. He'd dropped his sword and the man'd kicked it from the porch.

He felt himself being dragged back into the house. He tried to fight, but his body didn't listen. The dots began to fade into shapes. The man was tall and thin. He didn't look that strong, but Erik knew better. He grabbed Erik by the shirt and shoved him into a cage. He took a key from his pocket and locked him in.

The Stitch cowered in the corner, whimpering. The man strolled to it. He snatched a knife from the table and squatted. He grabbed the creature by the tusk and lifted its head. "You've made a horrible mess in here."

Nils' hands were bound, but his feet were free. Now was his chance to escape. What was he doing just standing there? Erik motioned toward the door, but Nils shook his head. Behind the door stood a deer with the head of a wolf. No escape was possible.

The Stitch in the corner gave a sharp cry and collapsed to the ground. The man replaced the knife on the table and walked back to the cage. Erik scampered back, but the man grabbed his face and pulled it against the bars. The man pushed his glasses back and squinted. Locking eyes with Erik, he examined the rest of his head, and flung it back.

"Where's the girl?" he asked.

Nils' head shot up.

Erik shook his head.

"No matter. It won't be long before my scout reports back to me. Don't get too comfy, I've got plans for you." He picked up the rope attached to Nils' arms and strolled to the door.

"The girl..." Nils said. "Are you talking about Pia?"

The man looked at Nils and rubbed his chin. "What does it matter to you?"

"My mom's sick. If I get the reward for bringing the girl back, I can help her."

"Why should I care about that?" the man asked.

"You're Rosaline's father, aren't you?" Nils asked. "Don't you know how it feels to lose someone who shouldn't have to die?"

The man's eyes widened. He tugged the ropes around Nils' hands and yanked him to the door. "You and I have some things to discuss." He waved and the Stitch at the door disappeared.

They left and Erik was alone. And like Ozzie, he sat staring at the knives on the table, wishing one were near.

Ozzie moved as quickly as he could, but with only one arm and a blind girl holding on to it, it was difficult. Vergis, on the other hand, flew so quickly that it was hard to keep up. Ozzie sped up, but stumbled on a root. He tumbled to the ground, pulling the girl down with him.

"Vergis, you have to slow down," Ozzie said. "We can't keep up."

Vergis perched on a branch and looked down at them. "We don't have time. If Erik doesn't kill the Stitch, then it'll catch us in no time, and you two wouldn't have much of a chance."

Ozzie pushed himself up. "I should be there helping him."

"No, the girl needs you to help her to safety."

"It's useless," the girl said. "There's no getting away from him. You shouldn't have even tried."

"It was the right thing to do," Ozzie said.

"No, she's right." Vergis dropped down to Ozzie and lowered his voice. "I'm certain we're being followed. He doesn't trust me anymore, but I have a plan. I'm going to lead you to the monastery. You two'll stay there, but I'm going to continue on to my cave."

Ozzie shook his head. "If you're being followed, won't they know you've left us?"

"No, I'll keep talking as I fly. The scout will think you're following me."

"It seems risky," Ozzie said.

"It is, but it's the best chance we've got."

"Why go to your cave?" the girl asked. "Why don't you lead it around in circles?"

"I don't have a choice," Vergis said. "Erik thinks we're going there. If he killed the Stitch and comes after us, that's where he'll go."

"Why don't you stay in the monastery and we'll wait for Erik in the cave?" Ozzie asked. "I know the way."

Vergis shook his head. "If the Stitcher captures Erik, he might torture him into telling the location of the cave. You'll be safer in the monastery."

He flew back to the branch above. "Let's go. We have to hurry."

Body parts. Next to Erik's cage was a small pile of severed legs. Wolf legs, deer legs, fox legs, and some he couldn't even identify. He clamped his nose, but it didn't seem to help. The Stitcher'd be back for him soon, then it'd be all over. At least he was able to buy some time for Ozzie. He could die happier knowing Ozzie was safe. It was only too bad he'd never get to say goodbye. He couldn't even remember the last thing he'd said to him. Tears welled in his eyes and he shook his head.

Under the pile of limbs something shimmered in the dim light. He couldn't remember *his* last words, but he remembered Ozzie's: Versteck. Could it be? Erik stretched his arm through the cage, pressing his face against the bars. He tugged on the metal and pulled it from under the pile. It was the same saw he'd used to cut the girl's cage. Ozzie must've hid it for the next poor soul to find.

It didn't take long before he cut through the bars and was free. The difficulty now would be escaping unnoticed. The deer-Stitch with the wolf head was surely nearby. It'd be a deadly combination.

He peered through the broken door. The porch was empty. The cold night air was quiet, with nothing but a faint breathing at the bottom of the stairs. He tiptoed on the floorboards and reached the railing. Below him was the Stitch he'd seen in the doorway. Wisps of cloud puffed from its mouth. Erik would have zero chance to outrun it, and even less in fighting, especially in his condition. But he had an idea. Get a knife, jump down, and crash into it like a tree crumbling to the ground.

He crept back into the room and took a long-bladed knife. Its tip was sharp, and that's exactly what he'd need to run it through the Stitch's head. He prowled back to the edge. It wouldn't be a long drop, but hopefully it'd be enough to break a leg or two if he missed with the blade.

The only problem was that the Stitch was gone.

He stepped back from the edge and turned around. He wasn't alone on the porch. The wolf's mouth curled in a snarl as if taking pleasure in fooling its prey. Erik stepped back, but there wasn't much room. It galloped at him. Erik gripped the knife and swung, but it ducked its head, swiveled, and kicked him with its hind legs. It was like being slammed with the legs of a ladder. He shot back, dropped his knife, and crashed through the railing, falling over the edge.

He slammed into the earth. When his head cracked against the ground, the sky shattered into shimmering blackness. His chest shot with pain and although he was still, he felt like he was spinning. The creature scampered down the stairs. It was over, but Erik smiled. At least Ozzie got out to safety.

His head fell to the side.

Something was shining in the grass. His vision sharpened. He couldn't believe it...

His sword! The Stitcher'd kicked it off the porch when he was captured. He grabbed it, but he wasn't in much condition to fight. He was too dizzy. He'd have to take a different approach.

He closed his eyes and took a full breath, relaxing his muscles. The creature stomped toward him and lowered its head. It breath was warm on Erik's face. It sniffed his face, but Erik swung and impaled the

Stitch's neck with the sword. It jolted up and shrieked. Erik sawed and jagged the blade through its flesh. It collapsed next to him, its head half-removed.

Blood drained from the creature and covered Erik's hands and sleeves.

Erik pushed himself up, but pain stabbed his head. He staggered forward. He wouldn't have much time. He needed to get to Vergis' cave.

Ozzie felt a whole lot less safe now that Vergis was gone, but he also didn't know what to do. The endgame of the plan was to get to the monastery. Well, they were there. Now what? His only consolation was that he wasn't alone. The girl's attitude hadn't changed much though. She still remarked that it was useless. Sooner or later they'd be back with the Stitcher, and it'd be worse than before.

Ozzie sat her down on a pew and rested himself. She held her neck with one hand and rested her cheek on the other. Rhythmically, she caressed her skin.

"What do you think we should do now?" Ozzie asked.

The girl shook her head. "It doesn't matter."

"What if we got out of Odenwald, though? What would you do?"

"What could I do? No one cares for me, right? At least the Stitcher fed me."

"How could you defend that monster? He's done nothing but kidnap and kill children."

"Didn't he save you by removing your arm?"

"Maybe he did, but maybe he was lying. Even if he did, it wasn't because he wanted to be nice to me. I mean, he locked us up in cages. That's not what good people do. Did he cut out your eyes to save you, too?"

"He didn't cut out my eyes," she said. "He promised to give me new ones so I could see."

Ozzie's stomach felt queasy. He bent over and pushed it with his hand. Why would the Stitcher want to give her new eyes? Better still, where would he get the eyes?

She continued, "He said he'd been waiting for the perfect ones—pale blue eyes, like the ocean mist."

Is that why he'd said Ozzie's "parts" were no good? Because his eyes didn't match? Ozzie's eyes weren't the right color, but he knew whose were— Erik's. "That's why he wants my brother. He wants to give you his eyes. Doesn't that bother you?"

The girl nodded. "I don't like it, but what can I do?"

"He risked his life to save you! Tell him you don't want them!"

"Don't you think I've tried that? It doesn't matter what I say."

She brushed her hair back from her shoulder. There was something like a strand on her skin. She covered it and resumed rubbing her neck.

"What are you playing with on your neck?"

Her fingers stopped. "I don't know. I just have this little bump. I've always had it."

Ozzie seized her hand and forced it away. She screamed, "Knock it off," and recoiled, swatting in front of her.

"Show me," he ordered.

"Stop being a jerk," she said.

"I risked my life to save you," Ozzie said. "Just let me see."

She harrumphed. "Fine." She rested her hands on her lap. Ozzie moved in to examine her neck. It was what he feared. There was thin stitching on her neck, with a little bit of twine sticking through.

"Are you a Stitch?" he asked.

The path to the cave took a toll on Erik's body. His legs had taken so much abuse that he could barely walk without limping. Running was basically out of the question, although if he'd had a Stitch chasing him, he might give it a shot anyway. But soon he'd be safe with his brother. He slipped in the cave. Vergis stood in the shadows, alone. His stomach sank. Where were Ozzie and the girl?

Vergis jumped up and glided to the entrance. "We're not safe here anymore. We have to go."

"What? Why? Where's Ozzie?"

He stood at the opening. "There're probably Stitches on their way here now. Let's go."

Erik shook his head and bent over, panting. He rubbed his calves. "Where's Ozzie?"

"At the monastery."

"You left him alone?"

"We don't have time to discuss that." Vergis flew out of the cave.

Ugh. Erik needed a rest. He needed his brother. He limped after Vergis. "Wait, I'm coming."

Vergis was perched on a rock. "They should be safe."

Erik breathed deep and nodded. "I'm done. I can't run anymore. Just go and keep Ozzie safe."

Vergis cleared his throat. "Hope deferred makes the heart sick, but a desire fulfilled is a tree of life."

Erik squatted and laid his head in his hands. "What's that supposed to mean?"

"You're weak now, but being with your brother will give you new strength."

Erik shook his head. "Just keep him safe for me."

"I'm not leaving you out here," Vergis said. "We live or die together now."

Damn bird! Vergis dying here wouldn't be any help to Ozzie. Erik sighed and stood up. "Fine. Let's go."

The sun peaked through the trees. Erik was thankful for the morning light. He and Vergis slipped into the monastery. The hall filled with warm colors from the stained glass, like sunlight through autumn leaves. It was abandoned, but there was a faint snoring. Erik found Ozzie sleeping in a dormitory. He roused his brother. Ozzie coughed and scuttled out of the sleeping niche. They went and woke the girl also. They sat together where the light rested on the floor.

Ozzie smirked. "You found the saw?"

Erik nodded. "Versteck."

"The Stitcher's probably aware that you've escaped by now," Vergis said. "He's no doubt putting all his efforts into finding us. It won't be safe for us here much longer."

The girl nodded. "You shouldn't have come for me. He'll punish us all the more for trying to escape."

"We just have to get out of the forest," Erik said. "We've got Vergis. He's a scout. He can lead us to safety." He knew they'd need Vergis to get out alive, but he also knew Vergis wouldn't do this.

Vergis cleared his throat. "There is a severe discipline for him who forsakes the way. You mustn't forget that the only way the nightmare ends is to kill the Stitcher."

Erik shook his head. "How're we gonna do that? Look at us! We're a scout, a blind girl, a one-armed boy and me? He's got an army of monsters!"

Vergis cleared his throat. "The iniquities of the wicked ensnare him, and he is caught in the toils of his sin."

Ozzie looked at Erik and shook his head. "What does that mean?"

"It's something he does," Erik said. "You'll get used to it. I think he means that the Stitcher is going to do something that causes his own destruction. Is that right?"

Vergis nodded. "He'll send out what's left of his Stitches to find us, and that'll make him vulnerable. This is our best chance to kill him."

Ozzie held his arm over his stomach, but it was the missing one that made Erik afraid. "I can't risk Ozzie getting captured again."

"Not killing the Stitcher *is* risking Ozzie getting caught again," Vergis said.

"No, he doesn't want Ozzie, he wants me," Erik said. "And for some reason he wants her."

"Hasn't he already gotten what he needs from her?" Vergis asked.

Ozzie spoke up. "You didn't know? He didn't take her eyes. He wants Erik's eyes *for* her."

Erik jolted. "He wants my what?"

The girl nodded. "I think he's been building me for a long time, but it's hard to remember everything right."

Vergis' eyes were wide. He looked as surprised as Erik. "She's a Stitch," Erik said. "That's why she doesn't know her name, like you, Vergis."

"She's the only human Stitch I've ever seen," Vergis said. He turned to the girl. "Why is he doing this?"

She shook her head. "I don't know. I don't even know who I am."

"Vergis had a clue to who he was in an image he saw in the back of his mind," Erik said. "Do you have something like that? A picture in your head?"

She sighed. "Even in my mind I don't see much."

Ozzie held his head. "I'm gonna lie down."

Vergis said, "It doesn't really matter right now. We need to discuss our plan. We have to get to him before he gets to us."

He was right, but maybe there was another way. "What if I just let the Stitcher take me?" Erik asked. "He would leave Ozzie alone after that, wouldn't he?"

"He's not just going to take your eyes," Vergis said. "He never lets anyone go. He'll kill you."

"I know. But look, you'll die if we kill the Stitcher. If I give myself up, Ozzie'll be safe. You'll be safe. And it doesn't sound like he wants to kill her either. So many people have died because of me already. Maybe I can give something back."

"I won't be safe," Vergis said. "He'll either kill me himself, or just let me die from my own diseased parts."

"Not if *you* give me to him," Erik said.

Vergis shook his head and cleared his throat. "Sometimes a way seems right, but the end leads to death. It is not better for you to die than the Stitcher."

Vergis may be right about that, but Erik had made up his mind. "It's not up to you what I do for my brother. His safety is more important to me than killing the Stitcher." Ozzie was reclining on the floor. Erik nudged him. "Ozzie, get up. We gotta get ready to go."

He didn't stir. Erik shook him. "Ozzie, get up!"

He was still.

"Vergis, what's wrong with him?" Erik asked.

Vergis hopped over to Ozzie and examined his stub. "The Stitcher must've poisoned him, like he did to me and the others."

"But why?" Erik asked.

"I'm not sure," he said. "Why would he poison him if he was more useful to him alive? Alive, he could draw you close?"

Erik's face flushed with warmth. That was it. "His arm. He sewed it onto that Stitch we killed. It said, 'him for you.'"

Vergis was still for a moment. "We had it all wrong. This is the trade he's offering: To heal your brother in exchange for you. But you can't trust him, Erik. He won't help him."

"Then what can I do?" Erik asked.

"Kill him," Vergis said.

"You don't get it, Vergis! If I kill him, how does that help Ozzie?"

Vergis was silent. No quotes, no ideas.

"What if…" the girl spoke up. "What if you threaten him with me?"

"What do you mean?" Erik asked.

"I'm special to him. Vergis said so himself. I'm the only human Stitch he's ever seen. I must be important to him, right? What if you trade me?"

"Why would you do that?" Erik asked.

"We'll never get out of here anyway. He'll punish me when he catches us, but not if he thinks you kidnapped me."

It might work. Erik could make the Stitcher heal Ozzie, but then what? Was there any chance Ozzie'd be able to get away? All he had to do was hold her captive for a few hours while he escaped. But would it work? What if the Stitcher called his bluff?

"What if he refused? I don't think I could actually hurt you," Erik said.

"Do you have any better ideas?" she asked.

ROSALINE

The fire warmed her skin. Erik and Vergis had built it just outside the monastery, but she didn't help. She couldn't. Being blind made her useless in a lot of ways, and she hated it. They hoped to draw out any Stitches in the area with the fire. They'd be gone long before any Stitch got there of course. Erik and Vergis were busy getting everything gathered, so she sat near the blaze.

The cracking and smoky smell of the fire kindled her memory, and the burning licks of the flames revived images in her mind like a phoenix rising from ashes. Her heart beat faster and her fingers quivered. She could almost see the fire itself, and it scared the hell out of her.

They had broken through the doors, and they had come for her. Rosaline had always appreciated being the daughter of a doctor. Her father had delivered babies, fixed broken legs, and cured all kinds of illnesses. He'd been a hero for the town of Wiesthal. That was until the outbreak that killed the mayor's son and a handful of others. Then they turned on him, turned on all of them. They blamed him for his failure to heal their children, but there *was* no cure. He'd even turned to unusual methods, involving the injection of animal parts, even on her.

Their cold stares turned to fire when she alone recovered from the disease. It was proof, to them, of her father's preferential treatment.

Since she was the one who survived the plague, she was the one dragged from the house. "Witchcraft" was just a useful charge to satisfy their indignation. Her father called out for mercy, but there was no reasoning with the angry mob. They stacked up wood into a pyre and tied her against a board. She saw her father pushing men and women out of his way, trying to get to her. But he was waylaid.

The mayor touched the torch to the pyre. She had screamed at him, but he never looked at her. The flames grew engulfing both the wood and her body. She locked eyes with her father, who'd been knocked to his knees.

She was jolted from her memory when Erik tied a rope around her waist. "I have to carry Ozzie, so you'll be tied to me," Erik said and pulled her up.

They were on their way to the Stitcher, only now she knew why she was so special to him.

She was his daughter.

Erik stumbled over the rocks. His brother hung over his right shoulder, then his left, heavy as a sack of rocks, and just as conscious. Vergis was overhead, scouting the area and keeping them safe, at least until he left. Once they were close enough to the farmhouse, he planned on acting as a decoy and returning to the fire, hopefully drawing any nearby Stitches to himself.

Vergis flew down to Erik. He whispered, "It's time. There's no turning back."

Erik nodded and laid Ozzie down near a fence.

"I'll lead the Stitches to the camp. Wait 'til nightfall. If you get out alive, go West," Vergis said. "If you continue on that path you'll come to Sicherheit. There's a rectory there. That's where I came from, and they took care of the last boy who escaped the Stitcher. They'll take care of you, too."

Sicherheit.

He'd have to remember the name of that town. Not because he'd be going himself, but if Ozzie made it out alive, he'd send him there. But success would be a lot harder if there were other Stitches around. "What if they don't follow you?" Erik asked.

"You'll be on your own, but I'll do my best to prevent that."

Erik nodded. "Thanks Vergis. You gave me a second chance to save Ozzie. I wish there were a way to save you too."

Vergis cleared his throat. "The souls of the righteous are in the hand of God, and no torment will ever touch them. In the eyes of the foolish they seem to have died, and their departure was thought to be an affliction, but they are at peace. I now know why the stained glass window stuck in my mind. The lamb with the flag is me. If our victory means my death, then so be it. But *you* shouldn't have to die. *He* should. Kill him for me. Kill him for my sister. Kill him for anyone else he might take in the future."

Erik's rock called out to him, but he didn't have a free hand. He didn't want to be responsible for Vergis' death, too, but that was out of his control. "Good luck," Erik said. Telling Vergis his plan didn't involve killing the Stitcher would only upset him, and it wouldn't change anything. Still, it felt wrong to hide it from him.

"Good luck," Vergis repeated and flew off.

The farmhouse loomed on top of the hill. Its shadow reached far into the forest. The sky was blood red. It was time. Ozzie lay unconscious beside the fence. Erik placed a blanket over him. He pulled out a knife and took the girl by the arm. It'd have to look real. He held the knife to her neck.

They climbed over the brush and onto the clearing. The yard was empty. The air was quiet. Vergis' plan worked. There were no Stitches to contend with.

They ascended the stairs. He pushed open the door. Flies buzzed in the heavy air and animal parts were strewn about. The cages were haphazard, but one of them was moved next to the butcher's table.

Nils was inside it.

His left hand and chest were bandaged and stained red. His right hand gripped a bar of the cage as he rocked back-and-forth like a swing in the wind.

"Who's there?" Nils' eyes squinted, but he didn't startle at all, almost as if he were expecting someone to drop in.

Erik skulked around the piles of limbs. He searched the shadows. The Stitcher wasn't there. "Don't worry, it's me, Erik. Where's the Stitcher?"

"Help me outa here first, then we can talk."

"Is he here?" Erik repeated.

"No, and I don't wanna wait around for him either. Get me outa here."

Erik crept to the cage and cut the bars. Nils' head lowered, never making eye contact. Once freed, he crawled out and took a couple of knives from the table.

"He's gone out with his last couple Stitches to hunt you down," Nils said.

That wasn't the plan. He was just supposed to send the Stitches after them. "I was hoping he was here," Erik said.

Nils harnessed the knives in straps on his belt. "Why?"

"He's poisoned Ozzie, and I was hoping to offer him a trade."

Nils' head cocked and he shot a glance at Erik. "You gonna offer him money? Trust me, it won't work, he's got more than he needs, and no use for it."

Erik shook his head. "No, not that kind of trade. I've got something he wants."

A voice came from behind. "What's that?"

Erik startled, then turned.

Ozzie stood hunched in the doorway, drooping with his arm on the doorpost.

"Ozzie, are you okay?" Erik asked.

Ozzie slumped in the doorway. "I'ma...I'm kinda dizzy. But I woke up all alone..."

Erik dashed over to him. He took Ozzie's arm and wrapped it over his shoulder. "We gotta hurry. You're very sick, but I won't let you die."

Nils' voice came from behind. "I'm coming with you."

"Why would you wanna do that?" Erik asked.

"He's got something I need."

The whole plan had gone to hell, but Erik was glad for the extra man, especially since he'd have to get past more damned monsters. "Fine, but you gotta follow my orders. Ozzie's life depends on it."

What was the Stitcher doing here?

The blaze had been dying, but Vergis dropped off enough branches to keep it smoldering for hours.

There'd been no sign of any Stitches and that had begun to worry him, but now he worried even more. Erik couldn't kill the Stitcher if he wasn't at the farmhouse. It was up to him now.

It wouldn't be easy. He was flanked on both sides by his greatest Stitches, the two-headed monstrosity and the only other scout he knew about. Still, there was no sense doing nothing. If he fled, they'd no doubt head back and find Erik, Ozzie, and the girl. They'd be no match for these three.

Vergis hid behind the fire. His enemies made no noise acknowledging his presence. He'd at least have one unexpected shot. A sturdy branch lay halfway in the flames. Its tip burned orange and red. He grabbed it in his talons. He'd only have one chance at this. His talons tightened around the wood.

"Take to the sky," the Stitcher ordered.

A flutter of wings echoed from the trees. His cover wouldn't last another minute.

He leapt through the fire toward the Stitcher. Vergis' fiery lance reflected in the Stitcher's glasses. One thrust in his neck would do it.

The Stitcher flung his hands up over his face and ducked. Vergis adjusted and dived, but it didn't work. The Stitcher's guard jumped and caught the firebrand in his mouth, splintering it out of Vergis' control. The other head snapped at Vergis' neck, but hc jolted to the side. Fortunately, Vergis kept his head attached to his body; unfortunately, he lost his balance and crashed to the dirt right at the Stitcher's boots.

He jumped to attention, but the Stitcher snatched him by the throat.

The Stitcher shot out a loud whistle and his scout returned from the air to his side. His left hand constricted around Vergis' throat, while his right hand produced a thin blade from his jacket.

"I've given you so much," the Stitcher said.

He was right. He'd given him diseased eyes, a ruined memory, and suffering to keep him obedient. He'd been given hell, and Vergis wanted to return the favor.

He ran the blade into Vergis' side and hollowed out an eye. Vergis gritted his teeth and restrained his cries. His breath vacillated as if he were drowning. The Stitcher's eyes focused on him. He was waiting for a reaction. He loved knowing his weak spot, but Vergis wouldn't give him the satisfaction.

Then the Stitcher did something strange. He smiled and released his grasp on him.

Vergis crashed to the ground. The wolves pounced at him, but the Stitcher held out his hand in dismissal. The saliva from their mouths fell in gobs to the ground. The smell of it mixed with smoke and Vergis choked into the dirt.

"You've always been a favorite of mine, you know. I could've killed you many times. But I didn't." He tossed the extracted eye in the air. Sprinkles of blood spiraled out as it made its way back to his hand. "In honor of your service, I've removed the last cancerous eye from your body. You never have to come back to me to be fixed again."

Vergis rose and stood upright on his talons. What was he doing? It didn't make sense. Was he free? Trusting a faithless man in a time of trouble is like a bad tooth or a foot that slips. The Stitcher's smile remained.

"That eye there," Vergis nodded toward the Stitcher's hand, "is the last?"

The smile on his face diminished into a smirk and a wrinkled brow. "Well, almost. As you know, each eye has a *twin*. There is one more, but not in you. Do you understand?" He nodded slightly at the eagle-Stitch.

"Why should I care about a corrupted eye in that one?" Vergis asked.

His smile was gone. "You used to care about *her*. Do you still not understand?" he said, waving the eye gently in his hand.

Her? Twin? Was *that* her? Was that his sister? Vergis nodded slowly. "I...I understand."

"So why not make a deal with me? Help me one last time, and I will remove the other eye. Both of you can live on together."

"How am I to know you'd keep your word?"

"There's no use seeking assurances. My generosity can be exhausted, and you're in no place to bargain. Either help me and be rewarded, or I'll use you and you'll have nothing to show for it. Besides, does not one of your sayings go this way: be not righteous overmuch, why should you destroy yourself?"

Vergis cringed. Like a lame man's legs, which hang useless, is a proverb in the mouth of fools. But there wasn't anything he could do about it. The Stitcher had offered him his choice of damnations: betrayal of Erik or of his sister.

The trouble was that the Stitcher really did know Vergis' weak spot.

Erik and Nils had their blades out. The forest was dark, and the terrain was jagged rocks. They crept ahead. Every tree was a danger, providing cover for the monsters. Erik's heart beat quickly, but he was glad he didn't have to carry Ozzie anymore. He and Rosaline walked together behind them. Ozzie's weakness was met with Rosaline's strength, and her blindness was helped by Ozzie. They were like Uncle Bauer and Krause when piss drunk. Alone they would fall flat on their faces, but together, they could manage to walk.

"I think it's safe to talk, but quietly," Nils said.

Erik doubted that, but they were sitting ducks anyway. "Fine. Are you sure you know where the Stitcher is?" Erik asked.

"He went to the fire you built."

"That's what I don't understand. How'd you know we built a fire?"

Nils scoffed and shook his head. "You wouldn't believe me if I told you."

Erik smirked. A scout must've told the Stitcher. "Let me guess, a bird told him."

Nils' head shot toward Erik and he nearly stumbled over a root. "How'd you know?"

Erik wasn't sure if he should tell him about Vergis or not. "Yeah, I've heard one talk. Did it tell the Stitcher about the fire?"

"Yes. He left with two Stitches: the flying one and the one with two wolf-heads."

"Why'd he leave you in the ca—"

Rosaline's voice came from behind. "Wait up! There's something wrong with Ozzie."

Erik rushed back to him. "What's wrong?"

Ozzie was still standing. His face was pale. "That's the one that took the Walter twins, isn't it? The one with the two heads?"

Nils answered. "That's right. My father and I, uh, we interviewed everyone who witnessed kidnappings 'round Odenwald. In Fulda, it was a couple boys. Their story spread pretty much everywhere. Probably because the witness wasn't just some bar-hound or homeless fool."

"Don't worry, Ozzie," Erik said. "I'll keep you safe."

"But why does he have to do this?" Ozzie asked.

"Everyone has their reasons," Nils answered. "Sometimes they hurt other people to get what they want."

Rosaline nodded. "It's because I'm special to him. Everything he's done has been for me."

The wind whistled through the trees. Swaying branches moaned and creaked. Erik stood in front of Ozzie, sword in front of him. The bushes were still.

"Don't forget that I'm your prisoner," Rosaline said. "I don't want him to think I joined with you. He'll punish me if he thinks that."

Erik agreed, but it worried him. Was she just playing a part? Would she betray them at the earliest convenience?

They crept on. Erik whispered to Nils, "We'll have to be on guard about the girl. She's afraid that the Stitcher will punish her for being with us."

Nils whispered back, "What do you think she'll do?"

"She might abandon us if we don't keep a close eye on her. If we lose her, the whole thing falls apart."

Nils scratched his chest and let out a grunt. The wound on his chest must've hurt. Erik knew his pain. His whole body had suffered trauma this trip.

Nils spoke, "Why's she so important? Shouldn't we be more afraid of the Stitches than keeping an eye on her? I mean if it's life or death, I gotta take care of my business over babysitting the blind girl."

Erik was afraid of the Stitches too, but unlike Nils, he didn't plan on leaving Odenwald. Saving Ozzie, even at the cost of his own life, was the only way to make things right. So many people had died because of him. "She's special to him. She's my only leverage. I lose her, I lose Ozzie. I'll help you kill the Stitches, but when it comes to the Stitcher, we have to leave him alive, at least until he heals Ozzie."

"You have to know you're outnumbered. I mean there's three of them and two of us..." He looked back. "They're really more of a liability than an asset. Do you really think this'll end right?"

Erik did the math, but Nils was wrong. He didn't know about Vergis, and now it'd be important that he did know. He didn't want Nils trying to kill the wrong Stitch. If Vergis was still alive, that made it a fair fight, at least as far as the numbers were concerned. He was right about Ozzie, though. Keeping him safe would be a problem, but the girl was his best weapon. His only weapon, really. "I forgot to tell you, we have a Stitch of our own, unless he's been killed since earlier today. He's a scout, probably like the one you saw."

Nils chortled. "A good Stitch? I've never heard of such a thing. Between it and the girl, you really are susceptible to betrayal."

Erik's face heated. "Don't you dare say anything bad about Vergis." His words broke his whisper. Erik's fist clenched. "If Vergis betrayed anyone, it was the Stitcher." His heart was pounding. He needed to calm down. It wasn't Nils' fault. There was no way he could've known about Vergis. Erik released his hand and shoved it in his pocket. Vergis' death, whether it had already come or was still to come, was his fault, too. He inhaled and slowly blew out the air. "I'm sorry," he whispered, "but no, he's not loyal to the Stitcher."

Nils nodded. "How will I know which scout is bad though?"

"The one that attacks us is bad."

Ozzie and the girl called out to them in a hushed tone. Erik and Nils stopped until the two had reached them. The girl pointed to her nose. A hint of ashes was in the air. The cracking of burning wood echoed like distant gunshots. The battlefield was near.

The war was coming.

BURNING

Two heads.

It attacked like a gust of wind. It came out of nowhere and returned to nowhere. The sun still crouched beneath the earth and the fire could only illuminate what didn't hide. The trees were massive and offered cover for the creature. But that could work both ways.

"Go for cover," Erik said, dashing for an oak, but he never made it. The monster mauled him to the ground. Its maw gnashed into Erik's wrist. He dropped his sword and cried out. He took a knife from his belt and swung, but it was gone again. He jumped to his feet clenching his arm. It was wet but felt like it was burning.

"Ozzie, bring the girl and stick close together," Erik said.

It lunged again and knocked Erik on his back. He tried to roll away, but was pinned in place. His arms were nailed down above his head. The creature's saliva dripped on his face. Erik turned his head away.

Ozzie charged the beast, but was ambushed by the second head. Ozzie slammed to the ground. It growled at him and snapped its teeth, but he kicked the wolf's snout. It shrieked and flailed back.

Erik rolled and rose to his feet. He retrieved a second knife from his belt and stabbed at the first head. It tore its flesh above its nose. It wailed and retreated into the darkness.

The girl screeched. Nils pulled her. He must've been trying to move her to safety, but she kept screaming. The Stitch emerged near Nils and rushed at him. He released the girl and dived behind a tree. She tripped over a root, left completely vulnerable.

Ozzie coughed. "Erik, help her!" Ozzie was still on the ground. His face was pale. Erik wanted to stay with him, but the girl was the only way to save him.

Erik sprinted and lunged, his knife high over his head. He came down on the creature, stabbing into its neck. He ripped and tore at the stitching, cutting down its neck.

The Stitch galloped and flung him to the ground. The first head hung sideways, half-torn from its body. The second head's teeth clenched as it growled. It prowled toward him.

Erik shouted, "Nils, Help!"

But Nils was nowhere.

Erik pushed himself up. The Stitch circled him, waiting for the perfect moment. Erik dashed backward. The Stitch pounced at him, knocking him to the ground. Its breath was hot on his wound. It pounded his stomach with its paw. Erik's breath burst out and he choked. He slashed at the creature, but nothing connected. Its teeth reflected red light from the fire. He flung the knife in desperation. The hilt cracked into its nose.

The creature relented enough for Erik to roll from under its paw. He tried to pull a knife from his belt, but he'd lost them all. There was nothing nearby, so he braced his back on a rock, coiled his legs, and lunged his heels at its face. Its nose snapped like a cob of corn.

Its shriek rattled in Erik's head. It lumbered back. Erik rose to his feet, but doubled over, coughing with each inhalation.

Nils emerged. He was near the girl, protecting her, but she screamed and ran.

"N...n...n..." It was all Erik could manage.

The Stitch regrouped and glared at Erik. Blood oozed from its bent nose, but its eyes were wild more with anger than pain. It tromped at him. Erik froze.

It crashed into him. Erik smashed into the rocks, sending a jolt down his back.

The Stitch plowed into the ground, rolled, and quivered.

But it didn't get up.

Ozzie stood next to him, his torso turned almost backward. His arm was taut, a knife held fast in his hand. Chunks of bloodied tissue and stitching lined the ground from him to the beast.

Erik struggled to his feet.

The creature's second head gushed blood, half-severed from its body.

Ozzie'd killed it!

Erik limped to Ozzie, whose face was white. His mouth was open.

Erik smiled, holding a hand to Ozzie's cheek.

Ozzie's eyes rolled back. The knife slipped from his hand and he crumbled to the ground.

The girl screamed again. She ran toward Erik, but tripped on the uneven earth. "Help me," she screamed.

Ozzie was unconscious. Erik swiped his knife and went to the girl, lifting her up.

Then *he* appeared.

The Stitcher stood in the light of the fire. His face was dark, silhouetted against the blaze. His hands were at his side. He held something, but it was all shadow.

Erik grabbed the girl and forced her in front of him, his knife held to her neck.

Nils joined them. Ozzie was unconscious behind them all.

Erik broke the silence. "I've got a bargain for you."

The Stitcher stood erect and adjusted his glasses. "And what do you have to bargain with?"

Erik squeezed the girl's arm, digging his fingers into her skin. She screeched and struggled, but he held the knife to her neck. He didn't want to hurt her, but it had to look real, so the pain had to be real.

The Stitcher inched forward. There was no line, not a single wrinkle of emotion in his face.

"What about her?" Erik said. "Wouldn't you like her back?"

"Do you really think you're capable of killing her?" he asked.

Erik grabbed the girl by the hair and yanked it to the side. Her arms flailed and her fingers spread as she screamed. Her neck was bare and Erik felt his knife pierce some of the stitching.

The Stitcher stopped and nodded. "Don't get too eager. Maybe it is worth our time to barter." He lifted the object in this hand. Vergis swayed like a pendulum by his neck. "The girl for the traitor."

Erik staggered back, his knife lowered an inch. "Vergis?"

"I'm already dead," Vergis said. "Don't let him f—"

The Stitcher shook Vergis. "Shut up!"

Erik gasped. He couldn't just let Vergis die. He'd saved his life. "Fine," Erik said, through gritted teeth, but he tightened the knife on the girl's neck.

"Release her," he said.

"No. There's only one way I'm letting her go."

The Stitcher throttled Vergis' throat. "And what's that?"

"Fix Ozzie and let him leave," Erik said. "Vergis, too."

The Stitcher narrowed his eyes and looked around. "Ozzie? Was that his name? And where is he? I don't see him."

"He's somewhere safe," Erik said. "So what's your decision?"

"And if I do, you'll give her back to me?" he said. "Is that all you have to offer?"

"Yes."

He laughed and shook his head.

The girl whispered to Erik. "He's gonna kill you as soon as he has me, you know?"

"Such a fool. You're in no place to be making demands," the Stitcher said. "Do it."

Do it? Do what? Was he calling the bluff?

"Let her go," Nils said. A cool metallic sensation slid along Erik's neck.

He stiffened. Nils grabbed Erik's hair and pulled his head firmly. "What are you doing?" Erik asked.

"No sudden moves. Let her go, and drop the knife," Nils said.

Erik constricted his hand around his knife. It burned his fingers. A quiver of a smile emerged on the Stitcher's face.

Erik whispered to Nils, "Why are you doing this?"

"Let her go," Nils repeated. A sharp pain shot in Erik's neck. Nils' knife had punctured him.

Erik gasped a quick breath and released both his hands. A small trail of blood ran down his neck. His knife dropped and clanked on a rock. The girl fell forward and stumbled to her knees.

Nils' knife retreated from Erik's neck and he shoved Erik away. "Keep your hands up and move back," Nils said, his knife pointing at Erik's chest.

Erik stepped back holding his neck. "What are you doing? I thought you were on our side."

Nils lifted up the girl. "Come with me."

"Nils! Stop! This is crazy!" Erik said.

He took her by the hand and led her toward the Stitcher.

"What are you doing?" she asked. "Why are you helping him?"

He shook her. "Shut up."

"How can you do this? What would your mother think?" Erik asked.

Nils' steps sputtered, then stopped. He turned toward Erik. His face was red and his eyes filled with angry tears. "Pia's dead, and there's no reward for bringing home a dead girl. You're using her to save your brother. I'm using her to save my mom. I'm just doing what I have to do to save her."

He turned back to the girl, but she had a surprise for him. She plunged her knife into his neck. He dropped his blade and fell backward.

"Nils!" Erik yelled out. The girl stood still.

The Stitcher swooped toward her.

Erik shouted, "Watch out!"

She flailed her knife around her. She screamed, "Stay away from me!"

The Stitcher stopped. "Rosa, put the knife down. You'll be perfect soon. Just come to me."

She held the knife in front of her, and turned her head slightly as if trying to hear. Her body heaved with her heavy breaths, and she flashed the blade in the direction of the slightest noise.

Nils' voice was an airy whisper. "Help me." He gasped and choked. He held his hands in front of him. They were drenched in his blood. He planted them over his neck, but the wound was deep.

Erik was stuck. He couldn't retrieve the girl because she might stab him, and if he called for her the Stitcher would know she wasn't his prisoner. It was coming apart, and Ozzie didn't have much time.

"If I'm so important," the girl said, "why'd you keep me in a cage like everyone else?"

The Stitcher inched closer to her. "For your own safety."

"Safety from what?" she asked.

"From everyone."

Before Erik could warn her, The Stitcher rushed in and grabbed her wrist. His smile was gone. His face was hard. The girl yelled. He twisted her arm and swept her feet. She crashed on the ground, dropping the knife, her arm twisted in his grip.

Nils gagged. "Erik! Help me!"

"Why are you doing this to me?" the girl asked. "I'm your daughter."

"Because you're not finished. They ruined you."

A heavy weight fell upon Erik's shoulder from behind. He jumped forward and turned around to see what it was.

Ozzie tumbled to the ground. He fell on the nub of his missing arm and gave out a shout. Ozzie was just trying to steady himself on his brother. His face was pale, with beads of sweat.

Erik ran to him and pulled him up. "I'm sorry," Erik stammered, "I thought you were a Stitch."

"What happened?" Ozzie asked.

Where to begin? There was no time. Ozzie's eyes were on Nils. "He turned on us," Erik said.

The Stitcher gazed at Erik and Ozzie. He shot a whistle.

A rush of wings descended. An eagle glided and dived into Ozzie's chest. He plummeted to the ground. The Stitch alighted on his neck. Its talons tightened over him.

Erik's belt was empty and the ground was desolate of weapons. He dug his hand into his pocket and found his rock. One quick throw and he could end that Stitch's miserable life.

The Stitcher crept forward holding both the girl and Vergis. "It's time to give up. There's only one thing you have that I need."

Erik nodded. "My eyes…" His grip tightened on his rock. There were two birds, and only one stone. He sighed. "You're right."

Vergis' breathing was labored. His eyes watched him.

The Stitch nested on Ozzie's throat, guarding him. Ozzie's strength was gone. His chest rose and fell slowly.

The rock was smooth in Erik's hand.

The Stitcher moved closer. "You've caused me a lot of trouble."

Ozzie or Vergis?

Erik withdrew his hand and launched his rock at the Stitcher. It smashed his face. His glasses shattered and flung from his head as he dropped Vergis and the girl. He staggered back, covering his face. The girl fell flat onto the ground, but Vergis bounced and darted toward Ozzie.

The Stitcher yelled, "You'll pay for that, you stupid bastard." He removed a knife from his cloak. Blood drained from one eye. His teeth clenched.

Erik restrained a smile. Eye for an eye, that one was for Vergis. He ran to Nils, but he wasn't breathing. He took his knife.

Rosaline scrambled and grabbed at the Stitcher. She punched and clawed at him. "I hate you," she screamed and kicked at his legs.

Erik charged at the Stitcher.

The Stitcher kicked the girl's face. She flattened against the ground, held her face, and rolled in the dirt, crying.

Erik plunged the knife into the Stitcher's stomach and shoved him back. The Stitcher tripped to the ground and pulled the knife from his body. He pushed himself up and bounded toward Erik.

Erik backed away. The Stitcher's good eye was crazed. The other was a red mess. He swung back catching Erik's arm and slicing into it. Blood sprayed out, but there was almost no sensation. There was no more pain, only survival.

Erik rushed at him and clawed at his stomach, but stumbled and fell on his face. His nose bashed into the ground, and he felt a hot rush. Blood flowed down his face, but that was the least of his problems. He pushed himself up, and there was the Stitcher's blade, centimeters from him. One eye was closed and bloody, but murder was in the other.

Erik tightened.

The Stitcher's good eye shot open and his mouth let out a gasp. He pulled back.

The girl's hands wrapped around his neck from behind, her fingers clawing into his throat. He coughed blood. His fingers trembled. The knife escaped from his hand.

There'd be no saving Ozzie, now. Erik had failed his brother. There was only one last thing to do. He rushed forward and rammed into the Stitcher. He tumbled backward and tripped over the girl. He cracked his head on the wood in the fire. The flames wrapped over the Stitcher's head. He didn't move and Erik didn't dare go near him.

The sun peeking at the horizon brought with it the full contours of the violence of the night.

The breeze was dead with the smell of burnt flesh. Nils' body was grey and surrounded by a pool of his own blood. There was stitching, blood, and death everywhere. Vergis was alive and stood over the motionless eagle.

And there was Ozzie.

Erik's hand burrowed into his pocket; it was empty.

He limped over to Ozzie. His face was pale and he had tears in his eyes. His breathing was thin. Erik knew what he'd done. He'd failed him. There was no one to heal him now. "I'm sorry, Ozzie," he said. "I couldn't save you."

Ozzie opened his mouth, but his words were just air. All he could do was nod. There was no panic in his eyes. Erik didn't understand.

"It's all my fault, Ozzie. It shoulda been me."

A tear trickled down Ozzie's face. He shook his head. The corner of his lips rose into a slight smile and he pointed past them. Erik's gaze followed and fell on the girl, who was crying near the dead fire. He looked back to Ozzie. Ozzie whispered, "Like Mom."

Erik's bag was almost as full now as when he first left. He had his mother's book, his map, his rope, some really dirty clothes, and a new addition—a pouch of gold coins. He and Rosaline slumped through the rocky terrain like snails. His legs were bruised, dry blood cracked on his face, and his neck and left arm were wrapped tight.

Like Mom. Ozzie's words echoed in Erik's mind, but still didn't make sense. How was Rosaline like Mom?

They moved west through Odenwald. He would follow Vergis' path for as long as he could, but not to Sicherheit. He had other plans.

Vergis had won the battle against the other scout, but he didn't rejoice. He didn't go with them, either. He said he wanted to spend his final days in the monastery. His order would've rejected him if he'd ever gone back, even while he was human. But there was no one to turn him away at the monastery. Erik didn't understand any of it. All he knew was that he missed his friend, really the only one he had left.

Erik wouldn't return to Steinau. He also wouldn't be going to Lohr, not without Ozzie. And he wouldn't be going to the seminary where Vergis'd studied. Vergis had told Erik that they'd welcome him there, just as they helped the boy who escaped, but there was a greater task left. He was going to Erbach, where Nils had lived.

Tucked inside a pocket in Nils' jacket had been a newspaper article. Nils' face was pale and sad. Like so much that happened in Odenwald, his quest wasn't supposed to end that way. Erik had Vergis read the article to him. It described a woman whose disease had driven her family and friends away. She'd become violent even to those she loved. But Nils, her son, had loved her to the end.

Erik'd been angry at Nils. But then he heard the story. He passed the trees of Odenwald in silence with Rosaline. He and Nils weren't really so different. Erik too bargained with the Stitcher, for Ozzie's life. He even threatened Rosaline. He was only bluffing of course, but he wondered if that was entirely true. Rosaline's neck did have a small scar from his knife. Nils had sacrificed everything for his mother, even if it meant doing the Stitcher's dirty work. Hadn't Erik done the same for Ozzie?

Erik took Nils' gold. Nils was right about the Stitcher. He had more than enough money himself. Erik took it also. There had to be someone in Erbach that could help Nils' mother, and Erik had the money to pay for it.

Rosaline held his hand as they traversed the forest. Sometimes she would cry, other times she was silent. He didn't know what to do about her. At least now her identity was clearer to her, but that probably made things worse. After all, how many girls help to kill their father? How many girls have fathers who were monsters? She was one of a kind, and not in an entirely good way. Even though she was a Stitch, he doubted that the Stitcher poisoned her like he did the others.

"What are we going to do?" she asked.

He shook his head. "I don't know. But I won't leave you." Ozzie'd refused to leave the forest without her, even if it meant going against Erik and running toward his own death. Erik couldn't leave her, not after all Ozzie'd sacrificed.

Like Mom.

Like being lifted up by wings to see the whole forest, it suddenly made sense. *Rosaline* wasn't like Mom, *Ozzie* was. His death wasn't for nothing. That's why he'd been smiling. He'd died for Rosaline like Mom died for him. He passed on the gift.

Erik smirked and allowed his eyes to water.

Through the branches and leaves Erik saw farmland. There were also houses and people in the streets. Erik's heart beat within his chest. They'd reached the edge of Odenwald. Erik jogged, pulling Rosaline with him over the roots. In the center of the town stood gallows. No one hanged from the noose, but it turned his stomach.

He let go of Rosaline and searched his pocket.

It was empty. He'd forgotten!

"What is it?" Rosaline asked.

He turned around. It wasn't too far away. He could go back.

"Erik, are you there?" Rosaline asked.

Erik removed his hand and took Rosaline's again. Her hand was warm and soft, quite unlike his rock. "It's gone."

If you enjoyed this book, please take the time to rate and review it on Amazon.com. For more information on other books by Ryan J Slattery, visit www.rjslattery.com.

Acknowledgments

A work of art is begun for the artist, but it is finished for the public. This book would never have been completed without the help of many. Thank you first to my wife, Molly Slattery, for encouraging me to finish this book during the busiest time of our lives. You have always been there to support me, no matter how crazy my ideas were.

I'd also like to thank my fellow author Chanacee Ruth-Killgore, who was my earliest source of feedback and encouragement in this endeavor.

If there were an award for most typos per paragraph, I'd undoubtedly be the reigning champion. So to my poor overworked proofreaders, Patricia Post and Ryan Sextro, I want to give a special thank you.

Thank you also to my beta-readers, who without compensation courageously volunteered to read the first book of an then-unpublished author and provide feedback. Thank you John Hale, Steve Murphy, and Tina Rak for providing constructive criticism without reservations. I didn't need an ego-stroking, and you all gave me what I needed to hear. Thank you for not sugar-coating.

Finally, thank you to my seventh-grade students. None of you ever seemed to doubt for a second that the book would be awesome. Your enthusiasm greatly encouraged me.

About Ryan J Slattery

Ryan J Slattery has written stories since the second grade. Most of his work has been fairy tales to read to his children. The Stitcher is his first novel. He was born in Saint Louis in 1983, where he lives with his wife and two children.